THE INHERITORS

BOOKS BY JOSEPH CONRAD

ALMAYER'S FOLLY
AN OUTCAST OF THE ISLANDS
THE NIGGER OF THE "NARCISSUS"
TALES OF UNREST
LORD JIM: A ROMANCE
YOUTH: A NARRATIVE
TYPHOON
FALK, AND OTHER STORIES
NOSTROMO: A TALE OF THE SEABOARD
THE MIRROR OF THE SEA
THE SECRET AGENT
A SET OF SIX
UNDER WESTERN EYES
A PERSONAL RECORD
'TWIXT LAND AND SEA
CHANCE
WITHIN THE TIDES
VICTORY
THE SHADOW-LINE
THE ARROW OF GOLD
THE RESCUE
NOTES ON LIFE AND LETTERS
THE ROVER
THE SHORTER TALES OF JOSEPH
  CONRAD
TALES OF HEARSAY
LAUGHING ANNE AND ONE DAY
  MORE (Two Plays)
SUSPENSE

With Ford Madox Ford (Hueffer)

ROMANCE: A NOVEL
THE INHERITORS: AN EXTRAVAGANT
  STORY
THE NATURE OF A CRIME

THE INHERITORS

AN EXTRAVAGANT STORY

By JOSEPH CONRAD
and F. M. HUEFFER

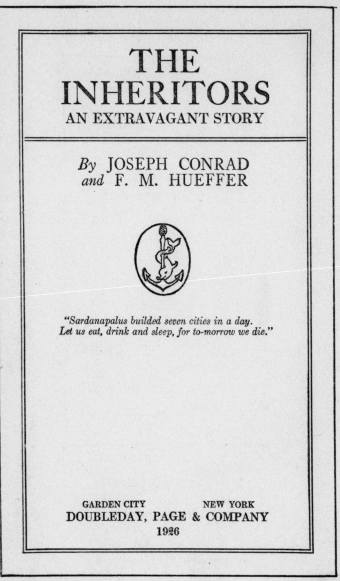

*"Sardanapalus builded seven cities in a day.
Let us eat, drink and sleep, for to-morrow we die."*

GARDEN CITY   NEW YORK
DOUBLEDAY, PAGE & COMPANY
1926

TO
BORYS AND CHRISTINA

THE INHERITORS

AN EXTRAVAGANT STORY

THE INHERITORS

CHAPTER ONE

"IDEAS," she said. "Oh, as for ideas——"

"Well?" I hazarded, "as for ideas——?"

We went through the old gateway and I cast a glance over my shoulder. The noon sun was shining over the masonry, over the little saints' effigies, over the little fretted canopies, the grime and the white streaks of bird-dropping.

"There," I said, pointing toward it, "doesn't that suggest something to you?"

She made a motion with her head—half negative, half contemptuous.

"But," I stuttered, "the associations—the ideas—the historical ideas——"

She said nothing.

"You Americans," I began, but her smile stopped me. It was as if she were amused at the utterances of an old lady shocked by the habits of the daughters of the day. It was the smile of a person who is confident of superseding one fatally.

(In conversations of any length one of the parties assumes the superiority—superiority of rank, intellectual or social. In this conversation she, if she did not attain to tacitly acknowledged temperamental superiority, seemed at least to claim it, to have no doubt as to its ultimate according. I was unused to this. I was a talker, proud of my conversational powers.

3

I had looked at her before; now I cast a sideways, critical glance at her. I came out of my moodiness to wonder what type this was. She had good hair, good eyes, and some charm. Yes. And something besides —a something—a something that was not an attribute of her beauty. The modelling of her face was so perfect and so delicate as to produce an effect of transparency, yet there was no suggestion of frailness; her glance had an extraordinary strength of life. Her hair was fair and gleaming, her cheeks coloured as if a warm light had fallen on them from somewhere. She was familiar till it occurred to you that she was strange.

"Which way are you going?" she asked.

"I am going to walk to Dover," I answered.

"And I may come with you?"

I looked at her—intent on divining her in that one glance. It was of course impossible. "There will be time for analysis," I thought.

"The roads are free to all," I said. "You are not an American?"

She shook her head. No. She was not an Australian either, she came from none of the British colonies.

"You are not English," I affirmed. "You speak too well." I was piqued. She did not answer. She smiled again and I grew angry. In the cathedral she had smiled at the verger's commendation of particularly abominable restorations, and that smile had drawn me toward her, had emboldened me to offer deferential and condemnatory remarks as to the plaster-of-Paris mouldings. You know how one addresses a young lady who is obviously capable of taking care of herself. That was how I had come across her. She had smiled at the gabble of the cathedral guide as he showed the obsessed troop, of which we had formed units, the place of martyrdom of Blessed Thomas, and her smile had had just that quality of superseder's contempt. It had pleased me then; but, now that she smiled thus past me—it was not quite at me—in the crooked highways of the town, I was irritated. After all, I was somebody; I was not a cathedral verger. I had a fancy for myself in those days—a fancy that solitude and brooding had crystallised into a habit of mind. I was a writer with high —with the highest—ideals. I had withdrawn myself from the world, lived isolated, hidden in the countryside, lived as hermits do, on the hope of one day doing something—of putting greatness on paper. She suddenly fathomed my thoughts: "You write," she affirmed. I asked how she knew, wondered what she had read of mine—there was so little.

"Are you a popular author?" she asked.

"Alas, no!" I answered. "You must know that."

"You would like to be?"

"We should all of us like," I answered; "though it is true some of us protest that we aim for higher things."

"I see," she said, musingly. As far as I could tell she was coming to some decision. With an instinctive dislike to any such proceeding as regarded myself, I tried to cut across her unknown thoughts.

"But, really—" I said, "I am quite a commonplace topic. Let us talk about yourself. Where do you come from?"

It occurred to me again that I was intensely unacquainted with her type. Here was the same smile— as far as I could see, exactly the same smile. (There are fine shades in smiles as in laughs, as in tones of voice.) I seemed unable to hold my tongue.

"Where do you come from?" I asked. "You must belong to one of the new nations. You are a foreigner, I'll swear, because you have such a fine contempt for us. You irritate me so that you might almost be a Prussian.

But it is obvious that you are of a new nation that is beginning to find itself."

"Oh, we are to inherit the earth, if that is what you mean," she said.

"The phrase is comprehensive," I said. I was determined not to give myself away. "Where in the world do you come from?" I repeated. The question, I was quite conscious, would have sufficed, but in the hope, I suppose, of establishing my intellectual superiority, I continued:

"You know, fair play's a jewel. Now I'm quite willing to give you information as to myself. I have already told you the essentials—you ought to tell me something. It would only be fair play."

"Why should there be any fair play?" she asked.

"What have you to say against that?" I said. "Do you not number it among your national characteristics?"

"You really wish to know where I come from?"

I expressed light-hearted acquiescence.

"Listen," she said, and uttered some sounds. I felt a kind of unholy emotion. It had come like a sudden, suddenly hushed, intense gust of wind through a breathless day. "What——what!" I cried.

"I said I inhabit the Fourth Dimension."

I recovered my equanimity with the thought that I had been visited by some stroke of an obscure and unimportant physical kind.

"I think we must have been climbing the hill too fast for me," I said, "I have not been very well. I missed what you said." I was certainly out of breath.

"I said I inhabit the Fourth Dimension," she repeated with admirable gravity.

"Oh, come," I expostulated, "this is playing it rather low down. You walk a convalescent out of breath and then propound riddles to him."

I was recovering my breath, and, with it, my inclination to expand. Instead, I looked at her. I was beginning to understand. It was obvious enough that she was a foreigner in a strange land, in a land that brought out her national characteristics. She must be of some race, perhaps Semitic, perhaps Sclav— of some incomprehensible race. I had never seen a Circassian, and there used to be a tradition that Circassian women were beautiful, were fair-skinned, and so on. What was repelling in her was accounted for by this difference in national point of view. One is, after all, not so very remote from the horse. What one does not understand one shies at—finds sinister, in fact. And she struck me as sinister.

"You won't tell me who you are?" I said.

"I have done so," she answered.

"If you expect me to believe that you inhabit a mathematical monstrosity, you are mistaken. You are, really."

She turned round and pointed at the city.

"Look!" she said.

We had climbed the western hill. Below our feet, beneath a sky that the wind had swept clean of clouds, was the valley; a broad bowl, shallow, filled with the purple of smoke-wreaths. And above the mass of red roofs there soared the golden stonework of the cathedral tower. It was a vision, the last word of a great art. I looked at her. I was moved, and I knew that the glory of it must have moved her.

She was smiling. "Look!" she repeated. I looked. There was the purple and the red, and the golden tower, the vision, the last word. She said something— uttered some sound.

What had happened? I don't know. It all looked contemptible. One seemed to see something beyond, something vaster—vaster than cathedrals, vaster than the conception of the gods to whom cathedrals were raised. The tower reeled out of the perpendicular. One saw beyond it, not roofs, or smoke, or hills, but an unrealized, an unrealizable infinity of space.

It was merely momentary. The tower filled its place again and I looked at her.

"What the devil," I said, hysterically—"what the devil do you play these tricks upon me for?"

"You see," she answered, "the rudiments of the sense are there."

"You must excuse me if I fail to understand," I said, grasping after fragments of dropped dignity. "I am subject to fits of giddiness." I felt a need for covering a species of nakedness. "Pardon my swearing," I added; a proof of recovered equanimity.

We resumed the road in silence. I was physically and mentally shaken; and I tried to deceive myself as to the cause. After some time I said:

"You insist then in preserving your—your incognito."

"Oh, I make no mystery of myself," she answered.

"You have told me that you come from the Fourth Dimension," I remarked, ironically.

"I come from the Fourth Dimension," she said, patiently. She had the air of one in a position of difficulty; of one aware of it and ready to brave it. She had the listlessness of an enlightened person who has to explain, over and over again, to stupid children some rudimentary point of the multiplication table.

She seemed to divine my thoughts, to be aware of their very wording. She even said "yes" at the opening of her next speech.

"Yes," she said. "It is as if I were to try to explain the new ideas of any age to a person of the age that has gone before." She paused, seeking a concrete illustra-

tion that would touch me. "As if I were explaining to
Dr. Johnson the methods and the ultimate vogue of the
cockney school of poetry."

"I understand," I said, "that you wish me to consider
myself as relatively a Choctaw. But what I do not
understand is: what bearing that has upon—upon the
Fourth Dimension, I think you said?"

"I will explain," she replied.

"But you must explain as if you were explaining to a
Choctaw," I said, pleasantly, "you must be concise and
convincing."

She answered: "I will."

She made a long speech of it; I condense. I can't
remember her exact words—there were so many; but
she spoke like a book. There was something exquisitely
piquant in her choice of words, in her expressionless
voice. I seemed to be listening to a phonograph recit-
ing a technical work. There was a touch of the
incongruous, of the mad, that appealed to me—the
commonplace rolling-down landscape, the straight,
white, undulating road that, from the tops of rises,
one saw running for miles and miles, straight, straight,
and so white. Filtering down through the great blue of
the sky came the thrilling of innumerable skylarks.
And I was listening to a parody of a scientific work re-
cited by a phonograph.

I heard the nature of the Fourth Dimension—heard
that it was an inhabited plane—invisible to our eyes,
but omnipresent; heard that I had seen it when Bell
Harry had reeled before my eyes. I heard the Dimensionists described; a race clear-sighted, eminently prac-
tical, incredible; with no ideals, prejudices, or remorse;
with no feeling for art and no reverence for life; free
from any ethical tradition; callous to pain, weakness,
suffering and death, as if they had been invulnerable

and immortal. She did not say that they were immortal, however. "You would—you will—hate us," she concluded. And I seemed only then to come to myself. The power of her imagination was so great that I fancied myself face to face with the truth. I supposed she had been amusing herself; that she should have tried to frighten me was inadmissible. I don't pretend that I was completely at my ease, but I said, amiably: "You certainly have succeeded in making these beings hateful."

"I have made nothing," she said with a faint smile, and went on amusing herself. She would explain origins, now.

"Your"—she used the word as signifying, I suppose, the inhabitants of the country, or the populations of the earth—"your ancestors were mine, but long ago you were crowded out of the Dimension as we are to-day, you overran the earth as we shall do to-morrow. But you contracted diseases, as we shall contract them,— beliefs, traditions; fears; ideas of pity . . . of love. You grew luxurious in the worship of your ideals, and sorrowful; you solaced yourselves with creeds, with arts —you have forgotten!"

She spoke with calm conviction; with an overwhelming and dispassionate assurance. She was stating facts; not professing a faith. We approached a little roadside inn. On a bench before the door a dun-clad country fellow was asleep, his head on the table.

"Put your fingers in your ears," my companion commanded.

I humoured her.

I saw her lips move. The countryman started, shuddered, and by a clumsy, convulsive motion of his arms, upset his quart. He rubbed his eyes. Before he had voiced his emotions we had passed on.

"I have seen a horse-coper do as much for a stallion," I commented. "I know there are words that have certain effects. But you shouldn't play pranks like the low-comedy devil in Faustus."

"It isn't good form, I suppose?" she sneered.

"It's a matter of feeling," I said, hotly, "the poor fellow has lost his beer."

"What's that to me?" she commented, with the air of one affording a concrete illustration.

"It's a good deal to him," I answered.

"But what to me?"

I said nothing. She ceased her exposition immediately afterward, growing silent as suddenly as she had become discursive. It was rather as if she had learnt a speech by heart and had come to the end of it. I was quite at a loss as to what she was driving at. There was a newness, a strangeness about her; sometimes she struck me as mad, sometimes as frightfully sane. We had a meal somewhere—a meal that broke the current of her speech—and then, in the late afternoon, took a by-road and wandered in secluded valleys. I had been ill; trouble of the nerves, brooding, the monotony of life in the shadow of unsuccess. I had an errand in this part of the world and had been approaching it deviously, seeking the normal in its quiet hollows, trying to get back to my old self. I did not wish to think of how I should get through the year—of the thousand little things that matter. So I talked and she—she listened very well.

But topics exhaust themselves and, at the last, I myself brought the talk round to the Fourth Dimension. We were sauntering along the forgotten valley that lies between Hardres and Stelling Minnis; we had been silent for several minutes. For me, at least, the silence was pregnant with the undefinable emotions that, at

times, run in currents between man and woman. The
sun was getting low and it was shadowy in those
shrouded hollows. I laughed at some thought, I forget
what, and then began to badger her with questions. I
tried to exhaust the possibilities of the Dimensionist
idea, made grotesque suggestions. I said: "And
when a great many of you have been crowded out of the
Dimension and invaded the earth you will do so and
so——" something preposterous and ironical. She
coldly dissented, and at once the irony appeared as
gross as the jocularity of a commercial traveller. Sometimes she signified: "Yes, that is what we shall do;"
signified it without speaking—by some gesture perhaps,
I hardly know what. There was something impressive
—something almost regal—in this manner of hers; it
was rather frightening in those lonely places, which were
so forgotten, so gray, so closed in. There was something
of the past world about the hanging woods, the little
veils of unmoving mist—as if time did not exist in those
furrows of the great world; and one was so absolutely
alone; anything might have happened. I grew weary
of the sound of my tongue. But when I wanted to
cease, I found she had on me the effect of some incredible stimulant.

We came to the end of the valley where the road
begins to climb the southern hill, out into the open air.
I managed to maintain an uneasy silence. From her
grimly dispassionate reiterations I had attained to a
clear idea, even to a visualisation, of her fantastic conception—allegory, madness, or whatever it was. She
certainly forced it home. The Dimensionists were to
come in swarms, to materialise, to devour like locusts,
to be all the more irresistible because indistinguishable.
They were to come like snow in the night: in the morning one would look out and find the world white; they

were to come as the gray hairs come, to sap the strength
of us as the years sap the strength of the muscles. As
to methods, we should be treated as we ourselves treat
the inferior races. There would be no fighting, no kill-
ing; we—our whole social system—would break as a
beam snaps, because we were worm-eaten with altruism
and ethics. We, at our worst, had a certain limit, a
certain stage where we exclaimed: "No, this is playing
it too low down," because we had scruples that acted
like handicapping weights. She uttered, I think, only
two sentences of connected words: "We shall race with
you and we shall not be weighted," and, "We shall
merely sink you lower by our weight." All the rest
went like this:

"But then," I would say . . . "we shall not be
able to trust any one. Any one may be one of you.
. . ." She would answer: "Any one." She prophe-
sied a reign of terror for us. As one passed one's
neighbour in the street one would cast sudden, piercing
glances at him.

I was silent. The birds were singing the sun down.
It was very dark among the branches, and from minute
to minute the colours of the world deepened and grew
sombre.

"But——" I said. A feeling of unrest was creeping
over me. "But why do you tell me all this?" I asked.
"Do you think I will enlist with you?"

"You will have to in the end," she said, "and I
do not wish to waste my strength. If you had to work
unwittingly you would resist and resist and resist. I
should have to waste my power on you. As it is, you
will resist only at first, then you will begin to understand. You will see how we will bring a man down—
a man, you understand, with a great name, standing for
probity and honour. You will see the nets drawing

closer and closer, and you will begin to understand.
Then you will cease resisting, that is all."

I was silent. A June nightingale began to sing, a
trifle hoarsely. We seemed to be waiting for some
signal. The things of the night came and went, rustled
through the grass, rustled through the leafage. At last
I could not even see the white gleam of her face. . . .

I stretched out my hand and it touched hers. I
seized it without an instant of hesitation. "How could
I resist you?" I said, and heard my own whisper with a
kind of amazement at its emotion. I raised her hand.
It was very cold and she seemed to have no thought of
resistance; but before it touched my lips something like
a panic of prudence had overcome me. I did not know
what it would lead to—and I remembered that I
did not even know who she was. From the beginning
she had struck me as sinister and now, in the obscurity,
her silence and her coldness seemed to be a passive
threatening of unknown entanglement. I let her hand
fall.

"We must be getting on," I said.

The road was shrouded and overhung by branches.
There was a kind of translucent light, enough to see her
face, but I kept my eyes on the ground. I was vexed.
Now that it was past the episode appeared to be a lost
opportunity. We were to part in a moment, and her
rare mental gifts and her unfamiliar, but very vivid,
beauty made the idea of parting intensely disagreeable.
She had filled me with a curiosity that she had done
nothing whatever to satisfy, and with a fascination that
was very nearly a fear. We mounted the hill and came
out on a stretch of soft common sward. Then the sound
of our footsteps ceased and the world grew more silent
than ever. There were little enclosed fields all around
us. The moon threw a wan light, and gleaming mist

hung in the ragged hedges.   Broad, soft roads ran away
into space on every side.

"And now . . ." I asked, at last, "shall we
ever meet again?"   My voice came huskily, as if I had
not spoken for years and years.

"Oh, very often," she answered.

"Very often?" I repeated.   I hardly knew whether
I was pleased or dismayed.   Through the gate-gap in a
hedge, I caught a glimmer of a white house front.   It
seemed to belong to another world; to another order of
things.

"Ah . . . here is Callan's," I said.   "This is
where I was going. . . ."

"I know," she answered; "we part here."

"To meet again?" I asked.

"Oh . . . to meet again; why, yes, to meet
again."

CHAPTER TWO

HER figure faded into the darkness, as pale things waver down into deep water, and as soon as she disappeared my sense of humour returned. The episode appeared more clearly, as a flirtation with an enigmatic, but decidedly charming, chance travelling companion. The girl was a riddle, and a riddle once guessed is a very trivial thing. She, too, would be a very trivial thing when I had found a solution. It occurred to me that she wished me to regard her as a symbol, perhaps, of the future—as a type of those who are to inherit the earth, in fact. She had been playing the fool with me, in her insolent modernity. She had wished me to understand that I was old-fashioned; that the frame of mind of which I and my fellows were the inheritors was over and done with. We were to be compulsorily retired; to stand aside superannuated. It was obvious that she was better equipped for the swiftness of life. She had a something—not only quickness of wit, not only ruthless determination, but a something quite different and quite indefinably more impressive. Perhaps it was only the confidence of the superseder, the essential quality that makes for the empire of the Occidental. But I was not a negro—not even relatively a Hindoo. I was somebody, confound it, I was somebody.

As an author, I had been so uniformly unsuccessful, so absolutely unrecognised, that I had got into the way of regarding myself as ahead of my time, as a worker for posterity. It was a habit of mind—the only revenge that I could take upon despiteful Fate. This girl came to confound me with the common herd—she declared herself to be that very posterity for which I worked.

She was probably a member of some clique that called themselves Fourth Dimensionists—just as there had been pre-Raphaelites. It was a matter of cant allegory. I began to wonder how it was that I had never heard of them. And how on earth had they come to hear of me!

"She must have read something of mine," I found myself musing: "the Jenkins story perhaps. It must have been the Jenkins story; they gave it a good place in their rotten magazine. She must have seen that it was the real thing, and. . . ." When one is an author one looks at things in that way, you know.

By that time I was ready to knock at the door of the great Callan. I seemed to be jerked into the commonplace medium of a great, great—oh, an infinitely great —novelist's home life. I was led into a well-lit drawing-room, welcomed by the great man's wife, gently propelled into a bedroom, made myself tidy, descended and was introduced into the sanctum, before my eyes had grown accustomed to the lamp-light. Callan was seated upon his sofa surrounded by an admiring crowd of very local personages. I forget what they looked like. I think there was a man whose reddish beard did not become him and another whose face might have been improved by the addition of a reddish beard; there was also an extremely moody dark man and I vaguely recollect a person who lisped.

They did not talk much; indeed there was very little conversation. What there was Callan supplied. He— spoke—very—slowly—and—very—authoritatively, like a great actor whose aim is to hold the stage as long as possible. The raising of his heavy eyelids at the opening door conveyed the impression of a dark, mental weariness; and seemed somehow to give additional length to his white nose. His short, brown beard was getting very gray, I thought. With his lofty forehead and with his superior, yet propitiatory smile, I was of course familiar. Indeed one saw them on posters in the street. The notables did not want to talk. They wanted to be spell-bound—and they were. Callan sat there in an appropriate attitude—the one in which he was always photographed. One hand supported his head, the other toyed with his watch-chain. His face was uniformly solemn, but his eyes were disconcertingly furtive. He cross-questioned me as to my walk from Canterbury; remarked that the cathedral was a—magnificent—Gothic—Monument and set me right as to the lay of the roads. He seemed pleased to find that I remembered very little of what I ought to have noticed on the way. It gave him an opportunity for the display of his local erudition.

"A—remarkable woman—used—to—live—in—the—cottage—next—the—mill—at—Stelling," he said; "she was the original of Kate Wingfield."

"In your 'Boldero?'" the chorus chorussed.

Remembrance of the common at Stelling—of the glimmering white faces of the shadowy cottages—was like a cold waft of mist to me. I forgot to say "Indeed!"

"She   was — a   very — remarkable — woman ——
She——"

I found myself wondering which was real; the common with its misty hedges and the blurred moon; or this room with its ranks of uniformly bound books and its bust of the great man that threw a portentous shadow upward from its pedestal behind the lamp.

Before I had entirely recovered myself, the notables were departing to catch the last train. I was left alone with Callan.

He did not trouble to resume his attitude for me, and when he did speak, spoke faster.

"Interesting man, Mr. Jinks?" he said; "you recognized him?"

"No," I said, "I don't think I ever met him."

Callan looked annoyed.

"I thought I'd got him pretty well. He's Hector Steele. In my 'Blanfield,'" he added.

"Indeed!" I said. I had never been able to read "Blanfield." "Indeed, ah, yes—of course."

There was an awkward pause.

"The whiskey will be here in a minute," he said, suddenly. "I don't have it in when What-not's here. He's the Rector, you know; a great temperance man. When we've had a—a modest quencher—we'll get to business."

"Oh," I said, "your letters really meant——"

"Of course," he answered. "Oh, here's the whiskey. Well now, Fox was down here the other night. You know Fox, of course?"

"Didn't he start the rag called——?"

"Yes, yes," Callan answered, hastily, "he's been very successful in launching papers. Now he's trying his hand with a new one. He's any amount of backers—big names, you know. He's to run my next as a *feuilleton*. This—this venture is to be rather more serious in tone than any that he's done hitherto. You understand?"

"Why, yes," I said; "but I don't see where I come in."

Callan took a meditative sip of whiskey, added a little more water, a little more whiskey, and then found the mixture to his liking.

"You see," he said, "Fox got a letter here to say that Wilkinson had died suddenly—some affection of the

heart. Wilkinson was to have written a series of personal articles on prominent people. Well, Fox was non-
plussed and I put in a word for you."

"I'm sure I'm much——" I began.

"Not at all, not at all," Callan interrupted, blandly.
"I've known you and you've known me for a number of
years."

A sudden picture danced before my eyes—the portrait of the Callan of the old days—the fawning, shady
individual, with the seedy clothes, the furtive eyes and
the obliging manners.

"Why, yes," I said; "but I don't see that that gives
me any claim."

Callan cleared his throat.

"The lapse of time," he said in his grand manner,
"rivets what we may call the bands of association."

He paused to inscribe this sentence on the tablets of
his memory. It would be dragged in—to form a purple
patch—in his new serial.

"You see," he went on, "I've written a good deal of
autobiographical matter and it would verge upon self-
advertisement to do more. You know how much I
dislike *that*. So I showed Fox your sketch in the
Kensington."

"The Jenkins story?" I said. "How did you come
to see it?"

"They send me the *Kensington*," he answered. There
was a touch of sourness in his tone, and I remembered
that the *Kensington* I had seen had been ballasted with
seven goodly pages by Callan himself—seven unreadable packed pages of a serial.

"As I was saying," Callan began again, "you ought
to know me very well, and I suppose you are acquainted
with my books. As for the rest, I will give you what
material you want."

"But, my dear Callan," I said, "I've never tried my hand at that sort of thing."

Callan silenced me with a wave of his hand.

"It struck both Fox and myself that your—your 'Jenkins' was just what was wanted," he said; "of course, that was a study of a kind of broken-down painter. But it was well done."

I bowed my head. Praise from Callan was best acknowledged in silence.

"You see, what we want, or rather what Fox wants," he explained, "is a kind of series of studies of celebrities *chez eux*. Of course, they are not broken down. But if you can treat them as you treated Jenkins—get them in their studies, surrounded by what in their case stands for the broken lay figures and the faded serge curtains— it will be exactly the thing. It will be a new line, or rather—what is a great deal better, mind you—an old line treated in a slightly, very slightly different way. That's what the public wants."

"Ah, yes," I said, "that's what the public wants. But all the same, it's been done time out of mind before. Why, I've seen photographs of you and your armchair and your pen-wiper and so on, half a score of times in the sixpenny magazines."

Callan again indicated bland superiority with a wave of his hand.

"You undervalue yourself," he said.

I murmured—"Thanks."

"This is to be—not a mere pandering to curiosity— but an attempt to get at the inside of things—to get the atmosphere, so to speak; not merely to catalogue furniture."

He was quoting from the prospectus of the new paper, and then cleared his throat for the utterance of a tremendous truth.

"Photography—is not—Art," he remarked.

The fantastic side of our colloquy began to strike me.

"After all," I thought to myself, "why shouldn't that girl have played at being a denizen of another sphere? She did it ever so much better than Callan. She did it too well, I suppose."

"The price is very decent," Callan chimed in. "I don't know how much per thousand, . . . but . . ."

I found myself reckoning, against my will as it were.

"You'll do it, I suppose?" he said.

I thought of my debts. . . . "Why, yes, I suppose so," I answered. "But who are the others that I am to provide with atmospheres?"

Callan shrugged his shoulders.

"Oh, all sorts of prominent people—soldiers, states-men, Mr. Churchill, the Foreign Minister, artists, preachers—all sorts of people."

"All sorts of glory," occurred to me.

"The paper will stand expenses up to a reasonable figure," Callan reassured me.

"It'll be a good joke for a time," I said. "I'm in-finitely obliged to you."

He warded off my thanks with both hands.

"I'll just send a wire to Fox to say that you accept," he said, rising. He seated himself at his desk in the appropriate attitude. He had an appropriate attitude for every vicissitude of his life. These he had struck before so many people that even in the small hours of the morning he was ready for the kodak wielder. Be-side him he had every form of labour-saver; every kind of literary knick-knack. There were book-holders that swung into positions suitable to appropriate attitudes; there were piles of little green boxes with red capital letters of the alphabet upon them, and big red boxes with black small letters. There was a writing-lamp that cast an æsthetic glow upon another appropriate attitude—and there was one typewriter with note-paper upon it, and another with MS. paper already in position.

"My God!" I thought—"to these heights the Muse soars."

As I looked at the gleaming pillars of the typewriters, the image of my own desk appeared to me; chipped, ink-stained, gloriously dusty. I thought that when again I lit my battered old tin lamp I should see ashes and match-ends; a tobacco-jar, an old gnawed penny pen-holder, bits of pink blotting-paper, match-boxes, old letters, and dust everywhere. And I knew that my atti-tude—when I sat at it—would be inappropriate.

Callan was ticking off the telegram upon his machine. "It will go in the morning at eight," he said.

CHAPTER THREE

To ENCOURAGE me, I suppose, Callan gave me the proof-sheets of his next to read in bed. The thing was so bad that it nearly sickened me of him and his jobs. I tried to read the stuff; to read it conscientiously, to read myself to sleep with it. I was under obligations to old Cal and I wanted to do him justice, but the thing was impossible. I fathomed a sort of a plot. It dealt in fratricide with a touch of adultery; a Great Moral Purpose loomed in the background. It would have been a dully readable novel but for that; as it was, it was intolerable. It was amazing that Cal himself could put out such stuff; that he should have the impudence. He was not a fool, not by any means a fool. It revolted me more than a little.

I came to it out of a different plane of thought. I may not have been able to write then—or I may; but I did know enough to recognise the flagrantly, the indecently bad, and, upon my soul, the idea that I, too, must cynically offer this sort of stuff if I was ever to sell my tens of thousands very nearly sent me back to my solitude. Callan had begun very much as I was beginning now; he had even, I believe, had ideals in his youth and had starved a little. It was rather trying to think that perhaps I was really no more than another Callan, that, when at last I came to review my life, I should have much such a record to look back upon. It disgusted me a little, and when I put out the light the horrors settled down upon me.

I woke in a shivering frame of mind, ashamed to meet

Callan's eye.   It was as if he must be aware of my over-
night thoughts, as if he must think me a fool who quarrelled with my victuals.   He gave no signs of any such
knowledge—was dignified, cordial; discussed his breakfast with gusto, opened his letters, and so on.   An
anæmic amanuensis was taking notes for appropriate
replies.   How could I tell him that I would not do
the work, that I was too proud and all the rest of it?
He would have thought me a fool, would have stiffened
into hostility, I should have lost my last chance.
And, in the broad light of day, I was loath to do
that.

He began to talk about indifferent things; we glided
out on to a current of mediocre conversation.   The
psychical moment, if there were any such, disappeared.

Someone bearing my name had written to express an
intention of offering personal worship that afternoon.
The prospect seemed to please the great Cal.   He was
used to such things; he found them pay, I suppose.   We
began desultorily to discuss the possibility of the writer's
being a relation of mine; I doubted.   I had no relations
that I knew of; there was a phenomenal old aunt who
had inherited the acres and respectability of the Etchingham Grangers, but she was not the kind of person to
worship a novelist.   I, the poor last of the family, was
without the pale, simply because I, too, was a novelist.
I explained these things to Callan and he commented on
them, found it strange how small or how large, I forget
which, the world was.   Since his own apotheosis shoals
of Callans had claimed relationship.

I ate my breakfast.   Afterward, we set about the
hatching of that article—the thought of it sickens me
even now.   You will find it in the volume along with the
others; you may see how I lugged in Callan's surround-
ings, his writing-room, his dining-room, the romantic

arbour in which he found it easy to write love-scenes, the clipped trees like peacocks and the trees clipped like bears, and all the rest of the background for appropriate attitudes. He was satisfied with any arrangements of words that suggested a gentle awe on the part of the writer.

"Yes, yes," he said once or twice, "that's just the touch, just the touch—very nice. But don't you think. . . ." We lunched after some time.

I was so happy. Quite pathetically happy. It had come so easy to me. I had doubted my ability to do the sort of thing; but it had written itself, as money spends itself, and I was going to earn money like that. The whole of my past seemed a mistake—a childishness. I had kept out of this sort of thing because I had thought it below me; I had kept out of it and had starved my body and warped my mind. Perhaps I had even damaged my work by this isolation. To understand life one must live—and I had only brooded. But, by Jove, I would try to live now.

Callan had retired for his accustomed siesta and I was smoking pipe after pipe over a confoundedly bad French novel that I had found in the book-shelves. I must have been dozing. A voice from behind my back announced:

"Miss Etchingham Granger!" and added—"Mr. Callan will be down directly." I laid down my pipe, wondered whether I ought to have been smoking when Cal expected visitors, and rose to my feet.

"You!" I said, sharply. She answered, "You see." She was smiling. She had been so much in my thoughts that I was hardly surprised—the thing had even an air of pleasant inevitability about it.

"You must be a cousin of mine," I said, "the name——"

"Oh, call it sister," she answered.

I was feeling inclined for farce, if blessed chance would throw it in my way. You see, I was going to live at last, and life for me meant irresponsibility.

"Ah!" I said, ironically, "you are going to be a sister to me, as they say." She might have come the bogy over me last night in the moonlight, but now . . . There was a spice of danger about it, too, just a touch lurking somewhere. Besides, she was good-looking and well set up, and I couldn't see what could touch me. Even if it did, even if I got into a mess, I had no relatives, not even a friend, to be worried about me. I stood quite alone, and I half relished the idea of getting into a mess—it would be part of life, too. I was going to have a little money, and she excited my curiosity. I was tingling to know what she was really at.

"And one might ask," I said, "what you are doing in this—in this. . . ." I was at a loss for a word to describe the room—the smugness parading as professional Bohemianism.

"Oh, I am about my own business," she said, "I told you last night—have you forgotten?"

"Last night you were to inherit the earth," I reminded her, "and one doesn't start in a place like this. Now I should have gone—well—I should have gone to some politician's house—a cabinet minister's—say to Gurnard's. He's the coming man, isn't he?"

"Why, yes," she answered, "he's the coming man."

You will remember that, in those days, Gurnard was only the dark horse of the ministry. I knew little enough of these things, despised politics generally; they simply didn't interest me. Gurnard I disliked platonically; perhaps because his face was a little enigmatic—a little repulsive. The country, then, was in the position of having no Opposition and a Cabinet

with two distinct strains in it—the Churchill and the
Gurnard—and Gurnard was the dark horse.

"Oh, you should join your flats," I said, pleasantly.
"If he's the coming man, where do you come in? . . .
Unless he, too, is a Dimensionist."

"Oh, both—both," she answered. I admired the
tranquillity with which she converted my points into
her own. And I was very happy—it struck me as a
pleasant sort of fooling. . . .

"I suppose you will let me know some day who you
are?" I said.

"I have told you several times," she answered.

"Oh, you won't frighten me to-day," I asserted,
"not here, you know, and anyhow, why should you
want to?"

"I have told you," she said again.

"You've told me you were my sister," I said; "but
my sister died years and years ago. Still, if it suits
you, if you want to be somebody's sister . . ."

"It suits me," she answered—"I want to be placed,
you see."

I knew that my name was good enough to place any
one. We had been the Grangers of Etchingham since
—oh, since the flood. And if the girl wanted to be my
sister and a Granger, why the devil shouldn't she, so
long as she would let me continue on this footing? I
hadn't talked to a woman—not to a well set-up one—
for ages and ages. It was as if I had come back from
one of the places to which younger sons exile themselves,
and for all I knew it might be the correct thing for girls
to elect brothers nowadays in one set or another.

"Oh, tell me some more," I said, "one likes to know
about one's sister. You and the Right Honourable
Charles Gurnard are Dimensionists, and who are the
others of your set?"

"There is only one," she answered. And would you believe it!—it seems he was Fox, the editor of my new paper.

"You select your characters with charming indiscriminateness," I said. "Fox is only a sort of toad, you know—he won't get far."

"Oh, he'll go far," she answered, "but he won't get there. Fox is fighting against us."

"Oh, so you don't dwell in amity?" I said. "You fight for your own hands."

"We fight for our own hands," she answered. "I shall throw Gurnard over when he's pulled the chestnuts out of the fire."

I was beginning to get a little tired of this. You see, for me, the scene was a veiled flirtation and I wanted to get on. But I had to listen to her fantastic scheme of things. It was really a duel between Fox, the Journal-founder, and Gurnard, the Chancellor of the Exchequer. Fox, with Churchill, the Foreign Minister, and his supporters, for pieces, played what he called "the Old Morality business" against Gurnard, who passed for a cynically immoral politician.

I grew more impatient. I wanted to get out of this stage into something more personal. I thought she invented this sort of stuff to keep me from getting at her errand at Callan's. But I didn't want to know her errand; I wanted to make love to her. As for Fox and Gurnard and Churchill, the Foreign Minister, who really was a sympathetic character and did stand for political probity, she might be uttering allegorical truths, but I was not interested in them. I wanted to start some topic that would lead away from this Dimensionist farce.

"My dear sister," I began. . . . Callan always moved about like a confounded eavesdropper, wore car-

pet slippers, and stepped round the corners of screens.
I expect he got copy like that.

"So, she's your sister?" he said suddenly, from behind me. "Strange that you shouldn't recognize the
handwriting. . . ."

"Oh, we don't correspond," I said light-heartedly,
"we are *so* different." I wanted to take a rise out of the
creeping animal that he was. He confronted her blandly.

"You must be the little girl that I remember," he said.
He had known my parents ages ago. That, indeed, was
how I came to know him; I wouldn't have chosen him
for a friend. "I thought Granger said you were dead
. . . but one gets confused. . . ."

"Oh, we see very little of each other," she answered.
"Arthur might have said I was dead—he's capable of
anything, you know." She spoke with an assumption
of sisterly indifference that was absolutely striking. I
began to think she must be an actress of genius, she
did it so well. She *was* the sister who had remained
within the pale; I, the rapscallion of a brother whose
vagaries were trying to his relations. That was the
note she struck, and she maintained it. I didn't
know what the deuce she was driving at, and I didn't
care. These scenes with a touch of madness appealed
to me. I was going to live, and here, apparently, was
a woman ready to my hand. Besides, she was making
a fool of Callan, and that pleased me. His patronising
manners had irritated me.

I assisted rather silently. They began to talk of
mutual acquaintances—as one talks. They both
seemed to know everyone in this world. She gave herself the airs of being quite in the inner ring; alleged
familiarity with quite impossible persons, with my
portentous aunt, with Cabinet Ministers—that sort of
people. They talked about them—she, as if she lived

among them; he, as if he tried very hard to live up to
them.

She affected reverence for his person, plied him with
compliments that he swallowed raw—horribly raw. It
made me shudder a little; it was tragic to see the little
great man confronted with that woman. It shocked
me to think that, really, I must appear much like him—
must have looked like that yesterday. He was a little
uneasy, I thought, made little confidences as if in spite
of himself; little confidences about the *Hour*, the new
paper for which I was engaged. It seemed to be run
by a small gang with quite a number of assorted axes
to grind. There was some foreign financier—a person
of position whom she knew (a noble man in the *best* sense,
Callan said); there was some politician (she knew him
too, and he was equally excellent, so Callan said), Mr.
Churchill himself, an artist or so, an actor or so—and
Callan. They all wanted a little backing, so it seemed.
Callan, of course, put it in another way. The Great—
Moral—Purpose turned up, I don't know why. He
could not think he was taking me in and she obviously
knew more about the people concerned than he did.
But there it was, looming large, and quite as farcical
as all the rest of it. The foreign financier—they called
him the Duc de Mersch—was by way of being a philanthropist on megalomaniac lines. For some international reason he had been allowed to possess himself
of the pleasant land of Greenland. There was gold in
it and train-oil in it and other things that paid—but
the Duc de Mersch was not thinking of that. He was
first and foremost a State Founder, or at least he was
that after being titular ruler of some little spot of a
Teutonic grand-duchy. No one of the great powers
would let any other of the great powers possess the
country, so it had been handed over to the Duc de

Mersch, who had at heart, said Cal, the glorious vision
of founding a model state—*the* model state in which
washed and broadclothed Esquimaux would live, side
by side, regenerated lives, enfranchised equals of
choicely selected younger sons of whatever occidental
race. It was that sort of thing. I was even a little
overpowered, in spite of the fact that Callan was its
trumpeter; there was something fine about the conception and Churchill's acquiescence seemed to guarantee
an honesty in its execution.

The Duc de Mersch wanted money, and he wanted
to run a railway across Greenland. His idea was that
the British public should supply the money and the
British Government back the railway, as they did in the
case of a less philanthropic Suez Canal. In return he
offered an eligible harbour and a strip of coast at one
end of the line; the British public was to be repaid in
casks of train-oil and gold and with the consciousness of
having aided in letting the light in upon a dark spot
of the earth. So the Duc de Mersch started the *Hour*.
The *Hour* was to extol the Duc de Mersch's moral
purpose; to pat the Government's back; influence
public opinion; and generally advance the cause of
the System for the Regeneration of the Arctic Regions.

I tell the story rather flippantly, because I heard it
from Callan, and because it was impossible to take
him seriously. Besides, I was not very much interested
in the thing itself. But it did interest me to see how
deftly she pumped him—squeezed him dry.

I was even a little alarmed for poor old Cal. After
all, the man had done me a service; had got me a job.
As for her, she struck me as a potentially dangerous
person. One couldn't tell, she might be some adventur-
ess, or if not that, a speculator who would damage Cal's
little schemes. I put it to her plainly afterward; and

quarrelled with her as well as I could. I drove her
down to the station. Callan must have been distinctly impressed or he would never have had out his
trap for her.

"You know," I said to her, "I won't have you play
tricks with Callan—not while you're using my name.
It's very much at your service as far as I'm concerned—
but, confound it, if you're going to injure him I shall
have to show you up—to tell him."

"You couldn't, you know," she said, perfectly calmly.
"You've let yourself in for it. He wouldn't feel pleased
with you for letting it go as far as it has. You'd lose
your job, and you're going to live, you know—you're
going to live. . . ."

I was taken aback by this veiled threat in the midst
of the pleasantry. It wasn't fair play—not at all fair
play. I recovered some of my old alarm, remembered
that she really was a dangerous person; that . . .

"But I sha'n't hurt Callan," she said, suddenly,
"you may make your mind easy."

"You really won't?" I asked.

"Really not," she answered. It relieved me to believe her. I did not want to quarrel with her. You
see, she fascinated me, she seemed to act as a stimulant,
to set me tingling somehow—and to baffle me. . . .
And there was truth in what she said. I had let myself
in for it, and I didn't want to lose Callan's job by telling
him I had made a fool of him.

"I don't care about anything else," I said. She
smiled.

CHAPTER FOUR

I WENT up to town bearing the Callan article, and a letter of warm commendation from Callan to Fox. I had been very docile; had accepted emendations; had lavished praise, had been unctuous and yet had contrived to retain the dignified savour of the editorial "we." Callan himself asked no more.

I was directed to seek Fox out—to find him immediately. The matter was growing urgent. Fox was not at the office—the brand new office that I afterward saw pass through the succeeding stages of business-like comfort and dusty neglect. I was directed to ask for him at the stage door of the Buckingham.

I waited in the doorkeeper's glass box at the Buckingham. I was eyed by the suspicious commissionaire with the contempt reserved for resting actors. Resting actors are hungry suppliants as a rule. Call-boys sought Mr. Fox. "Anybody seen Mr. Fox? He's gone to lunch."

"Mr. Fox is out," said the commissionaire.

I explained that the matter was urgent. More call-boys disappeared through the folding doors. Unenticing personages passed the glass box, casting hostile glances askance at me on my high stool. A message came back.

"If it's Mr. Etchingham Granger, he's to follow Mr. Fox to Mrs. Hartly's at once."

I followed Mr. Fox to Mrs. Hartly's—to a little flat in a neighbourhood that I need not specify. The eminent journalist was lunching with the eminent

actress. A husband was in attendance—a nonentity
with a heavy yellow moustache, who hummed and
hawed over his watch.

Mr. Fox was full-faced, with a persuasive, peremp-
tory manner. Mrs. Hartly was—well, she was just
Mrs. Hartly. You remember how we all fell in love
with her figure and her manner, and her voice, and the
way she used her hands. She broke her bread with
those very hands; spoke to her husband with that
very voice, and rose from table with that same graceful
management of her limp skirts. She made eyes at
me; at her husband; at little Fox, at the man who
handed the asparagus—great round gray eyes. She
was just the same. The curtain never fell on that
eternal dress rehearsal. I don't wonder the husband
was forever looking at his watch.

Mr. Fox was a friend of the house. He dispensed
with ceremony, read my manuscript over his Roque-
fort, and seemed to find it add to the savour.

"You are going to do me for Mr. Fox," Mrs. Hartly
said, turning her large gray eyes upon me. They were
very soft. They seemed to send out waves of intense
sympatheticism. I thought of those others that had
shot out a razor-edged ray.

"Why," I answered, "there was some talk of my
doing somebody for the *Hour*."

Fox put my manuscript under his empty tumbler.

"Yes," he said, sharply. "He will do, I think.
H'm, yes. Why, yes."

"You're a friend of Mr. Callan's, aren't you?" Mrs.
Hartly asked. "What a dear, nice man he is! You
should see him at rehearsals. You know I'm doing
his 'Boldero'; he's given me a perfectly lovely part—
perfectly lovely. And the trouble he takes. He tries
every chair on the stage."

"H'm; yes," Fox interjected, "he likes to have his own way."

"We *all* like that," the great actress said. She was quoting from her first great part. I thought—but, perhaps, I was mistaken—that all her utterances were quotations from her first great part. Her husband looked at his watch.

"Are you coming to this confounded flower show?" he asked.

"Yes," she said, turning her mysterious eyes upon him, "I'll go and get ready."

She disappeared through an inner door. I expected to hear the pistol-shot and the heavy fall from the next room. I forgot that it was not the end of the fifth act.

Fox put my manuscript into his breast pocket.

"Come along, Granger," he said to me, "I want to speak to you. You'll have plenty of opportunity for seeing Mrs. Hartly, I expect. She's tenth on your list. Good-day, Hartly."

Hartly's hand was wavering between his moustache and his watch pocket.

"Good-day," he said sulkily.

"You must come and see me again, Mr. Granger," Mrs. Hartly said from the door. "Come to the Buckingham and see how we're getting on with your friend's play. We must have a good long talk if you're to get my local colour, as Mr. Fox calls it."

> "To gild refined gold, to paint the lily,
>   To throw a perfume on the violet——"

I quoted banally.

"That's it," she said, with a tender smile. She was fastening a button of her glove. I doubt her recognition of the quotation.

When we were in our hansom, Fox began:

"I'm relieved by what I've seen of your copy. One didn't expect this sort of thing from you. You think it a bit below you, don't you? Oh, I know, I know. You literary people are usually so impracticable; you know what I mean. Callan said you were the man. Callan has his uses; but one has something else to do with one's paper. I've got interests of my own. But you'll do; it's all *right*. You don't mind my being candid, do you, now?" I muttered that I rather liked it.

"Well then," he went on, "now I see my way."

"I'm glad you do," I murmured. "I wish I did."

"Oh, that will be all right," Fox comforted. "I dare say Callan has rather sickened you of the job; particularly if you ain't used to it. But you won't find the others as trying. There's Churchill now, he's your next. You'll have to mind him. You'll find him a decent chap. Not a bit of side on him."

"What Churchill?" I asked.

"The Foreign Minister."

"The devil," I said.

"Oh, you'll find him all right," Fox reassured; "you're to go down to his place to-morrow. It's all arranged. Here we are. Hop out." He suited his own action to his words and ran nimbly up the new terra-cotta steps of the *Hour's* home. He left me to pay the cabman.

When I rejoined him he was giving directions to an invisible somebody through folding doors.

"Come along," he said, breathlessly. "Can't see him," he added to a little boy, who held a card in his hands. "Tell him to go to Mr. Evans. One's life isn't one's own here," he went on, when he had reached his own room.

It was a palatial apartment furnished in white and gold—Louis Quinze, or something of the sort—with very new decorations after Watteau covering the walls. The process of disfiguration, however, had already begun. A roll desk of the least possible Louis Quinze order stood in one of the tall windows; the carpet was marked by muddy footprints, and a matchboard screen had been run across one end of the room.

"Hullo, Evans," Fox shouted across it, "just see that man from Grant's, will you? Heard from the Central News yet?"

He was looking through the papers on the desk.

"Not yet, I've just rung them up for the fifth time," the answer came.

"Keep on at it," Fox exhorted.

"Here's Churchill's letter," he said to me. "Have an armchair; those blasted things are too uncomfortable for anything. Make yourself comfortable. I'll be back in a minute."

I took an armchair and addressed myself to the Foreign Minister's letter. It expressed bored tolerance of a potential interviewer, but it seemed to please Fox. He ran into the room, snatched up a paper from his desk, and ran out again.

"Read Churchill's letter?" he asked, in passing. "I'll tell you all about it in a minute." I don't know what he expected me to do with it—kiss the postage stamp, perhaps.

At the same time, it was pleasant to sit there idle in the midst of the hurry, the breathlessness. I seemed to be at last in contact with real life, with the life that matters. I was somebody, too. Fox treated me with a kind of deference—as if I were a great unknown. His "you literary men" was pleasing. It was the homage that the pretender pays to the legitimate prince; the recognition due to the real thing from the machine-made imitation; the homage of the builder to the architect.

"Ah, yes," it seemed to say, "we jobbing men run up our rows and rows of houses; build whole towns and fill the papers for years. But when we want something special—something monumental—we have to come to you."

Fox came in again.

"Very sorry, my dear fellow, find I can't possibly get a moment for a chat with you. Look here, come and dine with me at the Paragraph round the corner —to-night at six sharp. You'll go to Churchill's to-morrow."

The Paragraph Club, where I was to meet Fox, was one of those sporadic establishments that spring up in the neighbourhood of the Strand. It is one of their qualities that they are always just around the corner; another, that their stewards are too familiar; another, that they—in the opinion of the other members—are run too much for the convenience of one in particular.

In this case it was Fox who kept the dinner waiting. I sat in the little smoking-room and, from behind a belated morning paper, listened to the conversation of the three or four journalists who represented the members. I felt as a new boy in a school feels on his first introduction to his fellows.

There was a fossil dramatic critic sleeping in an arm-chair before the fire. At dinner-time he woke up, re-marked:

"You should have seen Fanny Ellsler," and went to sleep again.

Sprawling on a red velvet couch was a *beau jeune homme*, with the necktie of a Parisian-American student. On a chair beside him sat a personage whom, perhaps because of his plentiful lack of h's, I took for a distinguished foreigner.

They were talking about a splendid subject for a music-hall dramatic sketch of some sort—afforded by a bus driver, I fancy.

I heard afterward that my Frenchman had been a costermonger and was now half journalist, half financier, and that my art student was an employee of one of the older magazines.

"Dinner's on the table, gents," the steward said from the door. He went toward the sleeper by the fire. "I expect Mr. Cunningham will wear that arm-chair out before he's done," he said over his shoulder.

"Poor old chap; he's got nowhere else to go to," the magazine employee said.

"Why doesn't he go to the work'ouse," the journalist financier retorted. "Make a good sketch that, eh?" he continued, reverting to his bus driver.

"Jolly," the magazine employee said, indifferently.

"Now, then, Mr. Cunningham," the steward said, touching the sleeper on the shoulder, "dinner's on the table."

"God bless my soul," the dramatic critic said, with a start. The steward left the room. The dramatic critic furtively took a set of false teeth out of his waist-coat pocket, wiped them with a bandanna handkerchief, and inserted them in his mouth.

He tottered out of the room.

I got up and began to inspect the pen-and-ink sketches on the walls.

The faded paltry caricatures of faded paltry lesser lights that confronted me from fly-blown frames on the purple walls almost made me shiver.

"There you are, Granger," said a cheerful voice behind me. "Come and have some dinner."

I went and had some dinner. It was seasoned by small jokes and little personalities. A Teutonic journalist, a musical critic, I suppose, inquired as to the origin of the meagre pheasant. Fox replied that it had been preserved in the back-yard. The dramatic critic mumbled unheard that some piece or other was off the bills of the Adelphi. I grinned vacantly. Afterward, under his breath, Fox put me up to a thing or two regarding the inner meaning of the new daily. Put by him, without any glamour of a moral purpose, the case seemed rather mean. The dingy smoking-room depressed me and the whole thing was, what I had, for so many years, striven to keep out of. Fox hung over my ear, whispering. There were shades of intonation in his sibillating. Some of those "in it," the voice implied, were not above-board; others were, and the tone became deferential, implied that I was to take my tone from itself.

"Of course, a man like the Right Honourable C. does it on the straight, . . . quite on the straight, . . . has to have some sort of semi-official backer. . . . In this case, it's me, . . . the *Hour*. They're a bit splitty, the Ministry, I mean. . . . They say Gurnard isn't playing square . . . they *say* so." His broad, red face glowed as he bent down to my ear, his little sea-blue eyes twinkled with moisture. He enlightened me cautiously, circumspectly. There was something unpleasant in the business—not exactly in Fox himself, but the kind of thing. I wished he would cease his explanations—I didn't want to hear them. I have never wanted to know how things are worked; preferring to take the world at its face value. Callan's revelations had been bearable, because of the farcical pompousness of his manner. But this was different, it had the stamp of truth, perhaps because it was a little dirty. I didn't want to hear that the Foreign Minister was ever so remotely mixed up in this business. He was only a symbol to me, but he stood for the stability of statesmanship and for the decencies that it is troublesome to have touched.

"Of course," he was proceeding, "the Churchill gang would like to go on playing the stand-off to us. But it won't do, they've got to come in or see themselves left. Gurnard has pretty well nobbled their old party press, so they've got to begin all over again."

That was it—that was precisely it. Churchill ought to have played the stand-off to people like us—to have gone on playing it at whatever cost. That was what I demanded of the world as I conceived it. It was so much less troublesome in that way. On the other hand, this was life—I was living now and the cost of living is disillusionment; it was the price I had to pay. Obviously, a Foreign Minister had to have a semi-official organ, or I supposed so. . . . "Mind you," Fox whispered on, "I think myself, that it's a pity he is supporting the Greenland business. The thing's not *altogether* straight. But it's going to be made to pay like hell, and there's the national interest to be considered. If this Government didn't take it up, some other would— and that would give Gurnard and a lot of others a peg against Churchill and his. We can't afford to lose any more coaling stations in Greenland or anywhere else. And, mind you, Mr. C. can look after the interests of the niggers a good deal better if he's a hand in the pie. You see the position, eh?"

I wasn't actually listening to him, but I nodded at proper intervals. I knew that he wanted me to take that line in confidential conversations with fellows seeking copy. I was quite resigned to that. Incidentally, I was overcome by the conviction—perhaps it was no more than a sensation—that that girl was mixed up in this thing, that her shadow was somewhere among the others flickering upon the sheet. I wanted to ask Fox if he knew her. But, then, in that absurd business, I did not even know her name, and the whole story would have sounded a little mad. Just now, it suited me that Fox should have a moderate idea of my sanity. Besides, the thing was out of tone, I idealized her then. One wouldn't talk about her in a smoking-room full of men telling stories, and one wouldn't talk about her at all to Fox.

The musical critic had been prowling about the room with Fox's eyes upon him. He edged suddenly nearer, pushed a chair aside, and came toward us.

"Hullo," he said, in an ostentatiously genial, after-dinner voice, "what are you two chaps a-talking about?"

"Private matters," Fox answered, without moving a hair.

"Then I suppose I'm in the way?" the other muttered. Fox did not answer.

"Wants a job," he said, watching the discomfited Teuton's retreat, "but, as I was saying—oh, it pays both ways." He paused and fixed his eyes on me. He had been explaining the financial details of the matter, in which the Duc de Mersch and Callan and Mrs. Hartly and all these people clubbed together and started a paper which they hired Fox to run, which was to bring their money back again, which was to scratch their backs, which . . . It was like the house that Jack built; I wondered who Jack was. That was it, who was Jack? It all hinged upon that.

"Why, yes," I said. "It seems rather neat."

"Of course," Fox wandered on, "you are wondering why the deuce I tell you all this. Fact is, you'd hear it all if I didn't, and a good deal more that isn't true

besides. But I believe you're the sort of chap to respect a confidence."

I didn't rise to the sentiment. I knew as well as he
did that he was bamboozling me, that he was, as he said,
only telling me—not the truth, but just what I should
hear everywhere. I did not bear him any ill-will; it
was part of the game, that. But the question was, who
was Jack? It might be Fox himself. . . . There
might, after all, be some meaning in the farrago of nonsense that that fantastic girl had let off upon me. Fox
really and in a figure of speech such as she allowed herself, might be running a team consisting of the Duc de
Mersch and Mr. Churchill. He might really be backing a foreign, philanthropic ruler and State-founder
and a British Foreign Minister, against the rather sinister Chancellor of the Exchequer that Mr. Gurnard
undoubtedly was. It might suit him; perhaps he had
shares in something or other that depended on the success of the Duc de Mersch's Greenland Protectorate.
I knew well enough, you must remember, that Fox
was a big man—one of those big men that remain per-
manently behind the curtain, perhaps because they
have a certain lack of comeliness of one sort or another
and don't look well on the stage itself. And I understood now that if he had abandoned—as he had done—
half a dozen enterprises of his own for the sake of the
Hour, it must be because it was very well worth his
while. It was not merely a question of the editorship
of a paper; there was something very much bigger in
the background. My Dimensionist young lady, again,
might have other shares that depended on the Chancellor of the Exchequer's blocking the way. In that
way she might very well talk allegorically of herself
as in alliance with Gurnard against Fox and Churchill.
I was at sea in that sort of thing—but I understood

vaguely that something of the sort was remotely possible.

I didn't feel called upon to back out of it on that account, yet I very decidedly wished that the thing could have been otherwise. For myself, I came into the matter with clean hands—and I was going to keep my hands clean; otherwise, I was at Fox's disposal.

"I understand," I said, the speech marking my decision, "I shall have dealings with a good many of the proprietors—I am the scratcher, in fact, and you don't want me to make a fool of myself."

"Well," he answered, gauging me with his blue, gimlet eyes, "it's just as well to know."

"It's just as well to know," I echoed. It *was* just as well to know.

CHAPTER FIVE

I HAD gone out into the blackness of the night with a firmer step, with a new assurance. I had had my interview, the thing was definitely settled; the first thing in my life that had ever been definitely settled; and I felt I must tell Lea before I slept. Lea had helped me a good deal in the old days—he had helped everybody, for that matter. You would probably find traces of Lea's influence in the beginnings of every writer of about my decade; of everybody who ever did anything decent, and of some who never got beyond the stage of burgeoning decently. He had given me the material help that a publisher's reader could give, until his professional reputation was endangered, and he had given me the more valuable help that so few can give. I had grown ashamed of this one-sided friendship. It was, indeed, partly because of that that I had taken to the wilds—to a hut near a wood, and all the rest of what now seemed youthful foolishness. I had desired to live alone, not to be helped any more, until I could make *some* return. As a natural result I had lost nearly all my friends and found myself standing there as naked as on the day I was born.

All around me stretched an immense town—an immense blackness. People—thousands of people hurried past me, had errands, had aims, had others to talk to, to trifle with. But I had nobody. This immense city, this immense blackness, had no interiors for me. There were house fronts, staring windows, closed doors, but nothing within; no rooms, no hollow places. The

houses meant nothing to me, nothing more than the
solid earth. Lea remained the only one the thought
of whom was not like the reconsideration of an ancient,
a musty pair of gloves.

He lived just anywhere. Being a publisher's reader,
he had to report upon the probable commercial value
of the manuscripts that unknown authors sent to his
employer, and I suppose he had a settled plan of life,
of the sort that brought him within the radius of a given
spot at apparently irregular, but probably ordered,
intervals. It seemed to be no more than a piece of
good luck that let me find him that night in a little room
in one of the by-ways of Bloomsbury. He was sprawling angularly on a cane lounge, surrounded by whole
rubbish heaps of manuscript, a gray scrawl in a foam
of soiled paper. He peered up at me as I stood in the
doorway.

"Hullo!" he said, "what's brought you here? Have
a manuscript?" He waved an abstracted hand round
him. "You'll find a chair somewhere." A claret
bottle stood on the floor beside him. He took it by
the neck and passed it to me.

He bent his head again and continued his reading.
I displaced three bulky folio sheaves of typewritten
matter from a chair and seated myself behind him. He
continued to read.

"I hadn't seen these rooms before," I said, for want
of something to say.

The room was not so much scantily as arbitrarily
furnished. It contained a big mahogany sideboard;
a common deal table, an extraordinary kind of folding
wash-hand-stand; a deal bookshelf, the cane lounge,
and three unrelated chairs. There were three framed
Dutch prints on the marble mantel-shelf; striped curtains before the windows. A square, cheap looking-

glass, with a razor above it, hung between them. **And**
on the floor, on the chairs, on the sideboard, on the
unmade bed, the profusion of manuscripts.

He scribbled something on a blue paper and began to
roll a cigarette. He took off his glasses, rubbed them,
and closed his eyes tightly.

"Well, and how's Sussex?" he asked.

I felt a sudden attack of what, essentially, was nos-
talgia. The fact that I was really leaving an old course
of life, was actually and finally breaking with it, became vividly apparent. Lea, you see, stood for what
was best in the mode of thought that I was casting aside.
He stood for the aspiration. The brooding, the moodiness; all the childish qualities, were my own importa-
tions. I was a little ashamed to tell him, that—that
I was going to live, in fact. Some of the glory of it had
gone, as if one of two candles I had been reading by had
flickered out. But I told him, after a fashion, that I
had got a job at last.

"Oh, I congratulate you," he said.

"You see," I began to combat the objections he
had not had time to utter, "even for my work it will be
a good thing—I wasn't seeing enough of life to be able
to . . ."

"Oh, of course not," he answered—"it'll be a good
thing. You must have been having a pretty bad time."

It struck me as abominably unfair. I hadn't taken
up with the *Hour* because I was tired of having a bad
time, but for other reasons: because I had felt my soul
being crushed within me.

"You're mistaken," I said. And I explained. He
answered, "Yes, yes," but I fancied that he was adding
to himself—"They all say that." I grew more angry.
Lea's opinion formed, to some extent, the background
of my life. For many years I had been writing quite

as much to satisfy him as to satisfy myself, and his coldness chilled me. He thought that my heart was not in my work, and I did not want Lea to think that of me. I tried to explain as much to him—but it was difficult, and he gave me no help.

I knew there had been others that he had fostered, only to see them, in the end, drift into the back-wash. And now he thought I was going too . . .

"Here," he said, suddenly, breaking away from the subject, "look at that."

He threw a heavy, ribbon-bound mass of matter into my lap, and recommenced writing his report upon its saleability as a book. He was of opinion that it was too delicately good to attract his employer's class of readers. I began to read it to get rid of my thoughts. The heavy black handwriting of the manuscript sticks in my mind's eye. It must have been good, but probably not so good as I then thought it—I have entirely forgotten all about it; otherwise, I remember that we argued afterward: I for its publication; he against. I was thinking of the wretched author whose fate hung in the balance. He became a pathetic possibility, hidden in the heart of the white paper that bore pen-markings of a kind too good to be marketable. There was something appalling in Lea's careless—"Oh, it's too good!" He was used to it, but as for me, in arguing that man's case I suddenly became aware that I was pleading my own—pleading the case of my better work. Everything that Lea said of this work, of this man, applied to my work; and to myself. "There's no market for that sort of thing, no public; this book's been all round the trade. I've had it before. The man will never come to the front. He'll take to inn-keeping, and that will finish him off." That's what he said, and he seemed to be speaking of me. Someone was knocking at the door of the room—tentative knocks of rather flabby knuckles. It was one of those sounds that one does not notice immediately. The man might have been knocking for ten minutes. It happened to be Lea's employer, the publisher of my first book. He opened the door at last, and came in rather peremptorily. He had the air of having worked himself into a temper—of being intellectually rather afraid of Lea, but of being, for this occasion, determined to assert himself.

The introduction to myself—I had never met him—which took place after he had hastily brought out half a sentence or so, had the effect of putting him out of his stride, but, after having remotely acknowledged the possibility of my existence, he began again.

The matter was one of some delicacy. I myself should have hesitated to broach it before a third party, even one so negligible as myself. But Mr. Polehampton apparently did not. He had to catch the last post.

Lea, it appeared, had advised him to publish a manuscript by a man called Howden—a moderately known writer. . . .

"But I am disturbed to find, Mr. Lea, that is, my daughter tells me that the manuscript is not . . is not at all the thing. . . . In fact, it's quite—and—eh . . . I suppose it's too late to draw back?"

"Oh, it's altogether too late for *that*," Lea said, non-chalantly. "Besides, Howden's theories always sell."

"Oh, yes, of course, of course," Mr. Polehampton interjected, hastily, "but don't you think now . . . I mean, taking into consideration the damage it may do our reputation . . . that we ought to ask Mr. Howden to accept, say fifty pounds less than. . . ."

"I should think it's an excellent idea," Lea said.

Mr. Polehampton glanced at him suspiciously, then turned to me.

"You see," he began to explain, "one has to be *so* careful about these things."

"Oh, I can quite understand," I answered. There was something so naïve in the man's point of view that I had felt my heart go out to him. And he had taught me at last how it is that the godly grow fat at the expense of the unrighteous. Mr. Polehampton, however, was not fat. He was even rather thin, and his peaked gray hair, though it was actually well brushed, looked as if it ought not to have been. He had even an anxious expression. People said he speculated in some stock or other, and I should say they were right.

"I . . . eh . . . believe I published your first book . . . I lost money by it, but I can assure you that I bear no grudge—almost a hundred pounds. I bear no grudge . . ."

The man was an original. He had no idea that I might feel insulted; indeed, he really wanted to be pleasant, and condescending, and forgiving. I didn't feel insulted. He was too big for his clothes, gave that impression at least, and he wore black kid gloves. Moreover, his eyes never left the cornice of the room. I saw him rather often after that night, but never without his gloves and never with his eyes lowered.

"And . . . eh . . ." he asked, "what are you doing now, Mr. Granger?"

Lea told him Fox had taken me up; that I was going to go. I suddenly remembered it was said of Fox that everyone he took up did "go." The fact was obviously patent to Mr. Polehampton. He unbent with remarkable suddenness; it reminded me of the abrupt closing of a stiff umbrella. He became distinctly and crudely cordial—hoped that we should work together again;

once more reminded me that he had published my first book (the words had a different savour now), and was enchanted to discover that we were neighbours in Sussex. My cottage was within four miles of his villa, and we were members of the same golf club.

"We must have a game—several games," he said. He struck me as the sort of man to find a difficulty in getting any one to play with him.

After that he went away. As I had said, I did not dislike him—he was pathetic; but his tone of mind, his sudden change of front, unnerved me. It proved so absolutely that I was "going to go," and I did not want to go—in that sense. The thing is a little difficult to explain, I wanted to take the job because I wanted to have money—for a little time, for a year or so, but if I once began to go, the temptation would be strong to keep on going, and I was by no means sure that I should be able to resist the temptation. So many others had failed. What if I wrote to Fox, and resigned . . . Lea was deep in a manuscript once more.

"Shall I throw it up?" I asked suddenly. I wanted the thing settled.

"Oh, go on with it, by all means go on with it," Lea answered.

"And . . . ?" I postulated.

"Take your chance of the rest," he supplied; "you've had a pretty bad time."

"I suppose," I reflected, "if I haven't got the strength of mind to get out of it in time, I'm not up to much."

"There's that, too," he commented, "the game may not be worth the candle." I was silent. "You must take your chance when you get it," he added.

He had resumed his reading, but he looked up again when I gave way, as I did after a moment's thought.

"Of course," he said, "it will probably be all right.

You do your best. It's a good thing . . . might even do you good."

In that way the thing went through. As I was leaving the room, the idea occurred to me, "By the way, you don't know anything of a clique: the Dimensionists—*Fourth* Dimensionists?"

"Never heard of them," he negatived. "What's their specialty?"

"They're going to inherit the earth," I answered.

"Oh, I wish them joy," he closed.

"You don't happen to be one yourself? I believe it's a sort of secret society." He wasn't listening. I went out quietly.

The night effects of that particular neighbourhood have always affected me dismally. That night they upset me, upset me in much the same way, acting on much the same nerves as the valley in which I had walked with that puzzling girl. I remembered that she had said she stood for the future, that she was a symbol of my own decay—the whole silly farrago, in fact. I reasoned with myself—that I was tired, out of trim, and so on, that I was in a fit state to be at the mercy of any nightmare. I plunged into Southampton Row. There was safety in the contact with the crowd, in jostling, in being jostled.

CHAPTER SIX

IT WAS Saturday and, as was his custom during the session, the Foreign Secretary had gone for privacy and rest till Monday to a small country house he had within easy reach of town. I went down with a letter from Fox in my pocket, and early in the afternoon found myself talking without any kind of inward disturbance to the Minister's aunt, a lean, elderly lady, with a keen eye, and credited with a profound knowledge of European politics. She had a rather abrupt manner and a business-like, brown scheme of colouration. She looked people very straight in the face, bringing to bear all the penetration which, as rumour said, enabled her to take a hidden, but very real part in the shaping of our foreign policy. She seemed to catalogue me, label me, and lay me on the shelf, before I had given my first answer to her first question.

"You ought to know this part of the country well," she said. I think she was considering me as a possible canvasser—an infinitesimal thing, but of a kind possibly worth remembrance at the next General Election.

"No," I said, "I've never been here before."

"Etchingham is only three miles away."

It was new to me to be looked upon as worth consideration for my place-name. I realized that Miss Churchill accorded me toleration on its account, that I was regarded as one of the Grangers of Etchingham, who had taken to literature.

"I met your aunt yesterday," Miss Churchill continued. She had met everybody yesterday.

"Yes," I said, non-committally. I wondered what had happened at that meeting. My aunt and I had never been upon terms. She was a great personage in her part of the world, a great dowager landowner, as poor as a mouse, and as respectable as a hen. She was, moreover, a keen politician on the side of Miss Churchill. I, who am neither landowner, nor respectable, nor politician, had never been acknowledged—but I knew that, for the sake of the race, she would have refrained from enlarging on my shortcomings.

"Has she found a companion to suit her yet?" I said, absent-mindedly. I was thinking of an old legend of my mother's. Miss Churchill looked me in between the eyes again. She was preparing to relabel me, I think. I had become a spiteful humourist. Possibly I might be useful for platform malice.

"Why, yes," she said, the faintest of twinkles in her eyes, "she has adopted a niece."

The legend went that, at a hotly contested election in which my aunt had played a prominent part, a rainbow poster had beset the walls. "Who starved her governess?" it had inquired.

My accidental reference to such electioneering details placed me upon an excellent footing with Miss Churchill. I seemed quite unawares to have asserted myself a social equal, a person not to be treated as a casual journalist. I became, in fact, not the representative of the *Hour*—but an Etchingham Granger that competitive forces had compelled to accept a journalistic plum. I began to see the line I was to take throughout my interviewing campaign. On the one hand, I was "one of us," who had temporarily strayed beyond the pale; on the other, I was to be a sort of great author's bottle-holder.

A side door, behind Miss Churchill, opened gently.

There was something very characteristic in the tentative manner of its coming ajar. It seemed to say: "Why any noisy vigour?" It seemed to be propelled by a contemplative person with many things on his mind. A tall, gray man in the doorway leaned the greater part of his weight on the arm that was stretched down to the handle. He was looking thoughtfully at a letter that he held in his other hand. A face familiar enough in caricatures suddenly grew real to me—more real than the face of one's nearest friends, yet older than one had any wish to expect. It was as if I had gazed more intently than usual at the face of a man I saw daily, and had found him older and grayer than he had ever seemed before—as if I had begun to realize that the world had moved on.

He said, languidly—almost protestingly, "What am I to do about the Duc de Mersch?"

Miss Churchill turned swiftly, almost apprehensively, toward him. She uttered my name and he gave the slightest of starts of annoyance—a start that meant, "Why wasn't I warned before?" This irritated me; I knew well enough what were his relations with de Mersch, and the man took me for a little eavesdropper, I suppose. His attitudes were rather grotesque, of the sort that would pass in a person of his eminence. He stuck his eye-glasses on the end of his nose, looked at me short-sightedly, took them off and looked again. He had the air of looking down from an immense height —of needing a telescope.

"Oh, ah . . . Mrs. Granger's son, I presume. . . . I wasn't aware . . ." The hesitation of his manner made me feel as if we never should get anywhere—not for years and years.

"No," I said, rather brusquely, "I'm only from the *Hour*."

He thought me one of Fox's messengers then, said that Fox might have written: "Have saved you the trouble, I mean . . . or . . ."

He had the air of wishing to be amiable, of wishing, even, to please me by proving that he was aware of my identity.

"Oh," I said, a little loftily, "I haven't any message, I've only come to interview you." An expression of dismay sharpened the lines of his face.

"To . . ." he began, "but I've never allowed——" He recovered himself sharply, and set the glasses vigorously on his nose; at last he had found the right track. "Oh, I remember now," he said, "I hadn't looked at it in that way."

The whole thing grated on my self-love and I became, in a contained way, furiously angry. I was impressed with the idea that the man was only a puppet in the hands of Fox and de Mersch, and that lot. And he gave himself these airs of enormous distance. I, at any rate, was clean-handed in the matter; I hadn't any axe to grind.

"Ah, yes," he said, hastily, "you are to draw my portrait—as Fox put it. He sent me your Jenkins sketch. I read it—it struck a very nice note. And so——" He sat himself down on a preposterously low chair, his knees on a level with his chin. I muttered that I feared he would find the process a bore.

"Not more for me than for you," he answered, seriously—"one has to do these things."

"Why, yes," I echoed, "one has to do these things." It struck me that he regretted it—regretted it intensely; that he attached a bitter meaning to the words.

"And . . . what is the procedure?" he asked, after a pause. "I am new to the sort of thing." He had the air, I thought, of talking to some respectable

tradesman that one calls in only when one is *in extremis*
—to a distinguished pawnbroker, a man quite at the
top of a tree of inferior timber.

"Oh, for the matter of that, so am I," I answered.
"I'm supposed to get your atmosphere, as Callan put it."

"Indeed," he answered, absently, and then, after a
pause, "You know Callan?" I was afraid I should fall
in his estimation.

"One has to do these things," I said. "I've just been
getting his atmosphere."

He looked again at the letter in his hand, smoothed
his necktie and was silent. I realized that I was in the
way, but I was still so disturbed that I forgot how to
phrase an excuse for a momentary absence.

"Perhaps, . . ." I began.

He looked at me attentively.

"I mean, I think I'm in the way," I blurted out.

"Well," he answered, "it's quite a small matter.
But, if you are to get my atmosphere, we may as well
begin out of doors." He hesitated, pleased with his
witticism; "Unless you're tired," he added.

"I will go and get ready," I said, as if I were a lady
with bonnet-strings to tie. I was conducted to my
room, where I kicked my heels for a decent interval.
When I descended, Mr. Churchill was lounging about
the room with his hands in his trouser-pockets and his
head hanging limply over his chest. He said, "Ah!" on
seeing me, as if he had forgotten my existence. He
paused for a long moment, looked meditatively at himself in the glass over the fireplace, and then grew brisk.
"Come along," he said.

We took a longish walk through a lush home-country
meadow land. We talked about a number of things,
he opening the ball with that infernal Jenkins sketch.
I was in the stage at which one is sick of the thing, tired

THE INHERITORS

of the bare idea of it—and Mr. Churchill's laboriously kind phrases made the matter no better.

"You know who Jenkins stands for?" I asked. I wanted to get away on the side issues.

"Oh, I guessed it was——" he answered. They said that Mr. Churchill was an enthusiast for the school of painting of which Jenkins was the last exponent. He began to ask questions about him. Did he still paint? Was he even alive?

"I once saw several of his pictures," he reflected. "His work certainly appealed to me . . . yes, it appealed to me. I meant at the time . . . but one forgets; there are so many things." It seemed to me that the man wished by these detached sentences to convey that he had the weight of a kingdom—of several kingdoms—on his mind; that he could spare no more than a fragment of his thoughts for everyday use.

"You must take me to see him," he said, suddenly. "I ought to have something." I thought of poor white-haired Jenkins, and of his long struggle with adversity. It seemed a little cruel that Churchill should talk in that way without meaning a word of it—as if the words were a polite formality.

"Nothing would delight me more," I answered, and added, "nothing in the world."

He asked me if I had seen such and such a picture, talked of artists, and praised this and that man very fittingly, but with a certain timidity—a timidity that lured me back to my normally overbearing frame of mind. In such matters I was used to hearing my own voice. I could talk a man down, and, with a feeling of the unfitness of things, I talked Churchill down. The position, even then, struck me as gently humorous. It was as if some infinitely small animal were bullying some colossus among the beasts. I was of no account in the world, he had his say among the Olympians. And I talked recklessly, like any little school-master, and he swallowed it.

We reached the broad market-place of a little, red and gray, home county town; a place of but one street dominated by a great inn-signboard a-top of an enormous white post. The effigy of So-and-So of gracious memory swung lazily, creaking overhead.

"This is Etchingham," Churchill said.

It was a pleasant commentary on the course of time, this entry into the home of my ancestors. I had been without the pale for so long, that I had never seen the haunt of ancient peace. They had done very little, the Grangers of Etchingham—never anything but live at Etchingham and quarrel at Etchingham and die at Etchingham and be the monstrous important Grangers of Etchingham. My father had had the undesirable touch, not of the genius, but of the Bohemian. The Grangers of Etchingham had cut him adrift and he had swum to sink in other seas. Now I was the last of the Grangers and, as things went, was quite the best known of all of them. They had grown poor in their generation; they bade fair to sink, even as, it seemed, I bade fair to rise, and I had come back to the old places on the arm of one of the great ones of the earth. I wondered what the portentous old woman who ruled alone in Etchingham thought of these times—the portentous old woman who ruled, so they said, the place with a rod of iron; who made herself unbearable to her companions and had to fall back upon an unfortunate niece. I wondered idly who the niece could be; certainly not a Granger of Etchingham, for I was the only one of the breed. One of her own nieces, most probably. Churchill had gone into the post-office, leaving me standing at the foot of the sign-post. It was a pleasant summer day, the air very clear, the place very slumbrous. I looked up the street at a pair of great stone gate-posts, august, in their way, standing distinctly aloof from the common houses, a little weather-stained, staidly lich- ened. At the top of each column sat a sculptured wolf —as far as I knew, my own crest. It struck me pleas- antly that this must be the entrance of the Manor house.

The tall iron gates swung inward, and I saw a girl on a bicycle curve out, at the top of the sunny street. She glided, very clear, small, and defined, against the glow- ing wall, leaned aslant for the turn, and came shining down toward me. My heart leapt; she brought the whole thing into composition—the whole of that slum- brous, sunny street. The bright sky fell back into place, the red roofs, the blue shadows, the red and blue of the sign-board, the blue of the pigeons walking round my feet, the bright red of a postman's cart. She was glid- ing toward me, growing and growing into the central figure. She descended and stood close to me.

"You?" I said. "What blessed chance brought you here?"

"Oh, I am your aunt's companion," she answered, "her niece, you know."

"Then you *must* be a cousin," I said.

"No; sister," she corrected, "I assure you it's sister. Ask any one—ask your aunt." I was braced into a state of puzzled buoyancy.

"But really, you know," I said. She was smiling, standing up squarely to me, leaning a little back, sway- ing her machine with the motion of her body.

"It's a little ridiculous, isn't it?" she said.

"Very," I answered, "but even at that, I don't see ——And I'm not phenomenally dense."

"Not phenomenally," she answered.

"Considering that I'm not a—not a Dimensionist,"

I bantered. "But you have really palmed yourself off on my aunt?"

"Really," she answered, "she doesn't know any better. She believes in me immensely. I am such a real Granger, there never was a more typical one. And we shake our heads together over you." My bewilderment was infinite, but it stopped short of being unpleasant.

"Might I call on my aunt?" I asked. "It wouldn't interfere——"

"Oh, it wouldn't *interfere*," she said, "but we leave for Paris to-morrow. We are very busy. We—that is, my aunt; I am too young and too, too discreet—have a little salon where we hatch plots against half the régimes in Europe. You have no idea how Legitimate we are."

"I don't understand in the least," I said; "not in the least."

"Oh, you must take me literally if you want to understand," she answered, "and you won't do that. I tell you plainly that I find my account in unsettled states, and that I am unsettling them. Everywhere. You will see."

She spoke with her monstrous dispassionateness, and I felt a shiver pass down my spine, very distinctly. I was thinking what she might do if ever she became in earnest, and if ever I chanced to stand in her way—as her husband, for example.

"I wish you would talk sense—for one blessed minute," I said; "I want to get things a little settled in my mind."

"Oh, I'll talk sense," she said, "by the hour, but you won't listen. Take your friend, Churchill, now. He's the man that we're going to bring down. I mentioned it to you, and so . . ."

"But this is sheer madness," I answered.

"Oh, no, it's a bald statement of fact," she went on.

"I don't see how," I said, involuntarily.

"Your article in the *Hour* will help. Every trifle will help," she said. "Things that you understand and others that you cannot. . . . He is identifying himself with the Duc de Mersch. That looks nothing, but it's fatal. There will be friendships . . . and desertions."

"Ah!" I said. I had had an inkling of this, and it made me respect her insight into home politics. She must have been alluding to Gurnard, whom everybody —perhaps from fear—pretended to trust. She looked at me and smiled again. It was still the same smile; she was not radiant to-day and pensive to-morrow. "Do you know I don't like to hear that?" I began.

"Oh, there's irony in it, and pathos, and that sort of thing," she said, with the remotest chill of mockery in her intonation. "He goes into it clean-handed enough and he only half likes it. But he sees that it's his last chance. It's not that he's worn out—but he feels that his time has come—unless he does something. And so he's going to do something. You understand?"

"Not in the least," I said, light-heartedly.

"Oh, it's the System for the Regeneration of the Arctic Regions—the Greenland affair of my friend de Mersch. Churchill is going to make a grand coup with that—to keep himself from slipping down hill, and, of course, it would add immensely to your national prestige. And he only half sees what de Mersch is or *isn't*."

"This is all Greek to me," I muttered rebelliously.

"Oh, I know, I know," she said. "But one has to do these things, and I want you to understand. So Churchill doesn't like the whole business. But he's under the shadow. He's been thinking a good deal lately that

his day is over—I'll prove it to you in a minute—and so
—oh, he's going to make a desperate effort to get in
touch with the spirit of the times that he doesn't like
and doesn't understand. So he lets you get his atmosphere. That's all."

"Oh, that's *all*," I said, ironically.

"Of course he'd have liked to go on playing the stand-
off to chaps like you and me," she mimicked the tone
and words of Fox himself.

"This is witchcraft," I said. "How in the world
do you know what Fox said to me?"

"Oh, I know," she said. It seemed to me that she
was playing me with all this nonsense—as if she must
have known that I had a tenderness for her and were
fooling me to the top of her bent. I tried to get my
hook in.

"Now look here," I said, "we must get things settled.
You . . ."

She carried the speech off from under my nose.

"Oh, you won't denounce me," she said, "not any
more than you did before; there are so many reasons.
There would be a scene, and you're afraid of scenes—
and our aunt would back *me* up. She'd have to. My
money has been reviving the glories of the Grangers.
You can see, they've been regilding the gate."

I looked almost involuntarily at the tall iron gates
through which she had passed into my view. It was
true enough—some of the scroll work was radiant with
new gold.

"Well," I said, "I will give you credit for not wishing
to—to prey upon my aunt. But still . . ." I was
trying to make the thing out. It struck me that she
was an American of the kind that subsidizes households
like that of Etchingham Manor. Perhaps my aunt had
even forced her to take the family name, to save ap-

pearances. The old woman was capable of anything, even of providing an obscure nephew with a brilliant sister. And I should not be thanked if I interfered. This skeleton of swift reasoning passed between word and word . . . "You are no sister of mine!" I was continuing my sentence quite amiably.

Her face brightened to greet someone approaching behind me.

"Did you hear him?" she said. "*Did* you hear him, Mr. Churchill. He casts off—he disowns me. Isn't he a stern brother? And the quarrel is about nothing." The impudence—or the presence of mind of it—over-whelmed me.

Churchill smiled pleasantly.

"Oh—one always quarrels about nothing," Churchill answered. He spoke a few words to her; about my aunt; about the way her machine ran—that sort of thing. He behaved toward her as if she were an indulged child, impertinent with licence and welcome enough. He himself looked rather like the short-sighted, but in-dulgent and very meagre lion that peers at the unicorn across a plum-cake.

"So you are going back to Paris," he said. "Miss Churchill will be sorry. And you are going to continue to—to break up the universe?"

"Oh, yes," she answered, "we are going on with that; my aunt would never give it up. She couldn't, you know."

"You'll get into trouble," Churchill said, as if he were talking to a child intent on stealing apples. "And when is our turn coming? You're going to restore the Stuarts, aren't you?" It was his idea of badinage, amiable without consequence.

"Oh, not quite that," she answered, "not *quite* that." It was curious to watch her talking to another man—to a man, not a bagman like Callan. She put aside the face she always showed me and became at once what Churchill took her for—a spoiled child. At times she suggested a certain kind of American, and had that indefinable air of glib acquaintance with the names, and none of the spirit of tradition. One half expected her to utter rhapsodies about donjon-keeps.

"Oh, you know," she said, with a fine affectation of aloofness, "we shall have to be rather hard upon you; we shall crumple you up like—" Churchill had been moving his stick absent-mindedly in the dust of the road, he had produced a big "C H U." She had erased it with the point of her foot—"like that," she concluded.

He laid his head back and laughed almost heartily.

"Dear me," he said, "I had no idea that I was so much in the way of—of yourself and Mrs. Granger."

"Oh, it's not only that," she said, with a little smile and a cast of the eye to me. "But you've got to make way for the future."

Churchill's face changed suddenly. He looked rather old, and gray, and wintry, even a little frail. I understood what she was proving to me, and I rather disliked her for it. It seemed wantonly cruel to remind a man of what he was trying to forget.

"Ah, yes," he said, with the gentle sadness of quite an old man, "I dare say there is more in that than you think. Even you will have to learn."

"But not for a long time," she interrupted audaciously.

"I hope not," he answered, "I hope not." She nodded and glided away.

We resumed the road in silence. Mr. Churchill smiled at his own thoughts once or twice.

"A most amusing . . ." he said at last. "She does me a great deal of good, a great deal."

I think he meant that she distracted his thoughts.

"Does she always talk like that?" I asked. He had hardly spoken to me, and I felt as if I were interrupting a reverie—but I wanted to know.

"I should say she did," he answered; "I should *say* so. But Miss Churchill says that she has a real genius for organization. She used to see a good deal of them, before they went to Paris, you know."

"What are they doing there?" It was as if I were extracting secrets from a sleep-walker.

"Oh, they have a kind of a meeting place, for all kinds of Legitimist pretenders—French and Spanish, and that sort of thing. I believe Mrs. Granger takes it very seriously." He looked at me suddenly. "But you ought to know more about it than I do," he said.

"Oh, we see very little of each other," I answered, "you could hardly call us brother and sister."

"Oh, I see," he answered. I don't know what he saw. For myself, I saw nothing.

CHAPTER SEVEN

I succeeded in giving Fox what his journal wanted;
I got the atmosphere of Churchill and his house, in a
way that satisfied the people for whom it was meant.
His house was a pleasant enough place, of the sort where
they do you well, but not nauseously well. It stood
in a tranquil countryside, and stood there modestly.
Architecturally speaking, it was gently commonplace;
one got used to it and liked it. And Churchill himself,
when one had become accustomed to his manner, one
liked very well—very well indeed. He had a dainty,
dilettante mind, delicately balanced, with strong limita-
tions, a fantastic temperament for a person in his walk
of life—but sane, mind you, persistent. After a time,
I amused myself with a theory that his heart was not
in his work, that circumstance had driven him into the
career of politics and ironical fate set him at its head.
For myself, I had an intense contempt for the political
mind, and it struck me that he had some of the same
feeling. He had little personal quaintnesses, too, a
deference, a modesty, an open-mindedness.

I was with him for the greater part of his week-end
holiday; hung, perforce, about him whenever he had
any leisure. I suppose he found me tiresome—but one
has to do these things. He talked, and I talked; heav-
ens, how we talked! He was almost always deferential,
I almost always dogmatic; perhaps because the conversation kept on my own ground. Politics we never
touched. I seemed to feel that if I broached them, I
should be checked—politely, but very definitely. Per-

THE INHERITORS 69

haps he actually contrived to convey as much to me;
perhaps I evolved the idea that if I were to say:

"What do you think about the 'Greenland System'"
—he would answer:

"I try not to think about it," or whatever gently
closuring phrase his mind conceived. But I never did
so; there were so many other topics.

He was then writing his *Life of Cromwell* and his mind
was very full of his subject. Once he opened his heart,
after delicately sounding me for signs of boredom. It
happened, by the merest chance—one of those blind
chances that inevitably lead in the future—that I, too,
was obsessed at that moment by the Lord Oliver. A
great many years before, when I was a yearling of tremendous plans, I had set about one of those glorious
novels that one plans—a splendid thing with Old Noll
as the hero or the heavy father. I had haunted the
bookstalls in search of local colour and had wonderfully
well invested my half-crowns. Thus a company of
seventeenth century tracts, dog-eared, coverless, but
very glorious under their dust, accompany me through
life. One parts last with those relics of a golden age,
and during my late convalescence I had reread many of
them, the arbitrary half-remembered phrases suggesting
all sorts of scenes—lamplight in squalid streets, trays
full of weatherbeaten books. So, even then, my mind
was full of Mercurius Rusticus. Mr. Churchill on
Cromwell amused me immensely and even excited me.
It was life, this attending at a self-revelation of an
impossible temperament. It did me good, as he had
said of my pseudo-sister. It was fantastic—as fantastic as herself—and it came out more in his conversation
than in the book itself. I had something to do with
that, of course. But imagine the treatment accorded
to Cromwell by this delicate, negative, obstinately

judicial personality. It was the sort of thing one wants
to get into a novel. It was a lesson to me—in temperament, in point of view; I went with his mood, tried even
to outdo him, in the hope of spurring him to outdo himself. I only mention it because I did it so well that it
led to extraordinary consequences.

We were walking up and down his lawn, in the twilight, after his Sunday supper. The pale light shone
along the gleaming laurels and dwelt upon the soft
clouds of orchard blossoms that shimmered above them.
It dwelt, too, upon the silver streaks in his dark hair
and made his face seem more pallid, and more old. It
affected me like some intense piece of irony. It was
like hearing a dying man talk of the year after next.
I had the sense of the unreality of things strong upon
me. Why should nightingale upon nightingale pour
out volley upon volley of song for the delight of a politician whose heart was not in his task of keeping back
the waters of the deluge, but who grew animated at the
idea of damning one of the titans who had let loose the
deluge?

About a week after—or it may have been a fortnight
—Churchill wrote to me and asked me to take him to
see the Jenkins of my Jenkins story. It was one of
those ordeals that one goes through when one has tried
to advance one's friends. Jenkins took the matter
amiss, thought it was a display of insulting patronage
on the part of officialism. He was reluctant to show
his best work, the forgotten masterpieces, the things
that had never sold, that hung about on the faded walls
and rotted in cellars. He would not be his genial self;
he would not talk. Churchill behaved very well—I
think he understood.

Jenkins thawed before his gentle appreciations. I
could see the change operating within him. He began

to realize that this incredible visit from a man who ought to be hand and glove with Academicians was something other than a spy's encroachment. He was old, you must remember, and entirely unsuccessful. He had fought a hard fight and had been worsted. He took his revenge in these suspicions.

We younger men adored him. He had the ruddy face and the archaic silver hair of the King of Hearts; and a wonderful elaborate politeness that he had inherited from his youth—from the days of Brummell. And, whilst all his belongings were rotting into dust, he retained an extraordinarily youthful and ingenuous habit of mind. It was that, or a little of it, that gave the charm to my Jenkins story.

It was a disagreeable experience. I wished so much that the perennial hopefulness of the man should at last escape deferring and I was afraid that Churchill would chill before Jenkins had time to thaw. But, as I have said, I think Churchill understood. He smiled his kindly, short-sighted smile over canvas after canvas, praised the right thing in each, remembered having seen this and that in such and such a year, and Jenkins thawed.

He happened to leave the room—to fetch some studies, to hurry up the tea or for some such reason. Bereft of his presence the place suddenly grew ghostly. It was as if the sun had died in the sky and left us in that nether world where dead, buried pasts live in a gray, shadowless light. Jenkins' palette glowed from above a medley of stained rags on his open colour table. The rush-bottom of his chair resembled a wind-torn thatch.

"One can draw morals from a life like that," I said suddenly. I was thinking rather of Jenkins than of the man I was talking to.

"Why, yes," he said, absently, "I suppose there are men who haven't the knack of getting on."

"It's more than a knack," I said, with unnecessary bitterness. "It's a temperament."

"I think it's a habit, too. It may be acquired, mayn't it?"

"No, no," I fulminated, "it's precisely because it can't be acquired that the best men—the men like . . ." I stopped suddenly, impressed by the idea that the thing was out of tone. I had to assert myself more than I liked in talking to Churchill. Otherwise I should have disappeared. A word from him had the weight of three kingdoms and several colonies behind it, and I was forced to get that out of my head by making conversation a mere matter of temperament. In that I was the stronger. If I wanted to say a thing, I said it; but he was hampered by a judicial mind. It seemed, too, that he liked a dictatorial interlocutor, else he would hardly have brought himself into contact with me again. Perhaps it was new to him. My eye fell upon a couple of masks, hanging one on each side of the fireplace. The room was full of a profusion of little casts, thick with dust upon the shoulders, the hair, the eyelids, on every part that projected outward.

"By-the-bye," I said, "that's a death-mask of Cromwell."

"Ah!" he answered, "I know there *was* . . ."

He moved very slowly toward it, rather as if he did not wish to bring it within his field of view. He stopped before reaching it and pivoted slowly to face me.

"About my book," he opened suddenly, "I have so little time." His briskness dropped into a half complaint, like a faintly suggested avowal of impotence. "I have been at it four years now. It struck me—you seemed to coincide so singularly with my ideas."

His speech came wavering to a close, but he recommenced it apologetically—as if he wished me to help him out.

"I went to see Smithson the publisher about it, and he said he had no objection . . ."

He looked appealingly at me. I kept silence.

"Of course, it's not your sort of work. But you might try . . . You see . . ." He came to a sustained halt.

"I don't understand," I said, rather coldly, when the silence became embarrassing. "You want me to 'ghost' for you?"

"'Ghost,' good gracious no," he said, energetically; "dear me, no!"

"Then I really don't understand," I said.

"I thought you might see your . . . I wanted you to collaborate with me. Quite publicly, of course, as far as the epithet applies."

"To collaborate," I said slowly. "You . . ."

I was looking at a miniature of the Farnese Hercules —I wondered what it meant, what club had struck the wheel of my fortune and whirled it into this astounding attitude.

"Of course you must think about it," he said.

"I don't know," I muttered; "the idea is so new. It's so little in my line. I don't know what I should make of it."

I talked at random. There were so many thoughts jostling in my head. It seemed to carry me so much farther from the kind of work I wanted to do. I did not really doubt my ability—one does not. I rather regarded it as work upon a lower plane. And it was a tremendous—an incredibly tremendous—opportunity.

"You know pretty well how much I've done," he continued. "I've got a good deal of material together and a good deal of the actual writing is done. But there is ever so much still to do. It's getting beyond me, as I said just now."

I looked at him again, rather incredulously. He stood before me, a thin parallelogram of black with a mosaic of white about the throat. The slight grotesqueness of the man made him almost impossibly real in his abstracted earnestness. He so much meant what he said that he ignored what his hands were doing, or his body or his head. He had taken a very small, very dusty book out of a little shelf beside him, and was absently turning over the rusty leaves, while he talked with his head bent over it. What was I to him, or he to me?

"I could give my Saturday afternoons to it," he was saying, "whenever you could come down."

"It's immensely kind of you," I began.

"Not at all, not at all," he waived. "I've set my heart on doing it and, unless you help me, I don't suppose I ever shall get it done."

"But there are hundreds of others," I said.

"There may be," he said, "there may be. But I have not come across them."

I was beset by a sudden emotion of blind candour.

"Oh, nonsense, nonsense," I said. "Don't you see that you are offering me the chance of a lifetime?"

Churchill laughed.

"After all, one cannot refuse to take what offers," he said. "Besides, your right man to do the work might not suit me as a collaborator."

"It's very tempting," I said.

"Why, then, succumb," he smiled.

I could not find arguments against him, and I succumbed as Jenkins re-entered the room.

CHAPTER EIGHT

AFTER that I began to live, as one lives; and for forty-nine weeks. I know it was forty-nine, because I got fifty-two atmospheres in all; Callan's and Churchill's, and those forty-nine and the last one that finished the job and the year of it. It was amusing work in its way; people mostly preferred to have their atmospheres taken at their country houses—it showed that they had them, I suppose. Thus I spent a couple of days out of every week in agreeable resorts, and people were very nice to me—it was part of the game.

So I had a pretty good time for a year and enjoyed it, probably because I had had a pretty bad one for several years. I filled in the rest of my weeks by helping Fox and collaborating with Mr. Churchill and adoring Mrs. Hartly at odd moments. I used to hang about the office of the *Hour* on the chance of snapping up a blank three lines fit for a subtle puff of her. Sometimes they were too hurried to be subtle, and then Mrs. Hartly was really pleased.

I never understood her in the least, and I very much doubt whether she ever understood a word I said. I imagine that I must have talked to her about her art or her mission—things obviously as strange to her as to the excellent Hartly himself. I suppose she hadn't any art; I am certain she hadn't any mission, except to be adored. She walked about the stage and one adored her, just as she sat about her flat and was adored, and there the matter ended.

As for Fox, I seemed to suit him—I don't in the least

know why. No doubt he knew me better than I knew myself. He used to get hold of me whilst I was hanging about the office on the chance of engaging space for Mrs. Hartly, and he used to utilize me for the ignoblest things. I saw men for him, scribbled notes for him, abused people through the telephone, and wrote articles. Of course, there were the pickings.

I never understood Fox—not in the least, not more than I understood Mrs. Hartly. He had the manner-isms of the most incredible vulgarian and had, appar-ently, the point of view of a pig. But there was some-thing else that obscured all that, that forced one to call him a *wonderful* man. Everyone called him that. He used to say that he knew what he wanted and that he got it, and that was true, too. I didn't in the least want to do his odd jobs, even for the ensuing pickings, and I didn't want to be hail-fellow with him. But I did them and I was, without even realizing that it was distasteful to me. It was probably the same with everybody else.

I used to have an idea that I was going to reform him; that one day I should make him convert the *Hour* into an asylum for writers of merit. He used to let me have my own way sometimes—just often enough to keep my conscience from inconveniencing me. He let me pre-sent Lea with an occasional column and a half; and once he promised me that one day he would allow me to get the atmosphere of Arthur Edwards, the novelist.

Then there was Churchill and the *Life of Cromwell* that progressed slowly. The experiment succeeded well enough, as I grew less domineering and he less em-barrassed. Toward the end I seemed to have become a familiar inmate of his house. I used to go down with him on Saturday afternoons and we talked things over in the train. It was, to an idler like myself, wonderful the way that essential idler's days were cut out and fitted in like the squares of a child's puzzle; little passages of work of one kind fitting into quite unrelated passages of something else. He did it well, too, without the remotest semblance of hurry.

I suppose that actually the motive power was his aunt. People used to say so, but it did not appear on the surface to any one in close contact with the man; or it appeared only in very small things. We used to work in a tall, dark, pleasant room, book-lined, and giving on to a lawn that was always an asylum for furtive thrushes. Miss Churchill, as a rule, sat half forgotten near the window, with the light falling over her shoulder. She was always very absorbed in papers; seemed to be spending laborious days in answering letters, in evolving reports. Occasionally she addressed a question to her nephew, occasionally received guests that came informally but could not be refused admittance. Once it was a semi-royal personage, once the Duc de Mersch, my reputed employer.

The latter, I remember, was announced when Churchill and I were finally finishing our account of the tremendous passing of the Protector. In that silent room I had a vivid sense of the vast noise of the storm in that twilight of the crowning mercy. I seemed to see the candles a-flicker in the eddies of air forced into the gloomy room; the great bed and the portentous uncouth form that struggled in the shadows of the hangings. Miss Churchill looked up from the card that had been placed in her hands.

"Edward," she said, "the Duc de Mersch."

Churchill rose irritably from his low seat. "Confound him," he said, "I won't see him."

"You can't help it, I think," his aunt said, reflectively; "you will have to settle it sooner or later."

I know pretty well what it was they had to settle—
the Greenland affair that had hung in the air so long.
I knew it from hearsay, from Fox, vaguely enough. Mr.
Gurnard was said to recommend it for financial reasons,
the Duc to be eager, Churchill to hang back unaccount-
ably. I never had much head for details of this sort,
but people used to explain them to me—to explain the
reasons for de Mersch's eagerness. They were rather
shabby, rather incredible reasons, that sounded too reasonable to be true. He wanted the money for his railways—wanted it very badly. He was vastly in want
of money, he was this, that, and the other in certain
international-philanthropic concerns, and had a finger
in this, that, and the other pie. There was an "All
Round the World Cable Company" that united hearts
and hands, and a "Pan-European Railway, Exploration,
and Civilization Company" that let in light in dark
places, and an "International Housing of the Poor
Company," as well as a number of others. Somewhere
at the bottom of these seemingly bottomless concerns,
the Duc de Mersch was said to be moving, and the
Hour certainly contained periodically complimentary
allusions to their higher philanthropy and dividend-
earning prospects. But that was as much as I knew.
The same people—people one met in smoking-rooms—
said that the Trans-Greenland Railway was the last
card of de Mersch. British investors wouldn't trust the
Duc without some sort of guarantee from the British
Government, and no other investor would trust him on
any terms. England was to guarantee something or
other—the interest for a number of years, I suppose. I
didn't believe them, of course—one makes it a practice
to believe nothing of the sort. But I recognized that
the evening was momentous to somebody—that Mr.
Gurnard and the Duc de Mersch and Churchill were to

discuss something and that I was remotely interested because the *Hour* employed me.

Churchill continued to pace up and down.

"Gurnard dines here to-night," his aunt said.

"Oh, I see." His hands played with some coins in his trouser-pockets. "I see," he said again, "they've . . ."

The occasion impressed me. I remember very well the manner of both nephew and aunt. They seemed to be suddenly called to come to a decision that was no easy one, that they had wished to relegate to an indefinite future.

She left Churchill pacing nervously up and down.

"I could go on with something else, if you like," I said.

"But I don't like," he said, energetically; "I'd much rather not see the man. You know the sort of person he is."

"Why, no," I answered, "I never studied the Almanac de Gotha."

"Oh, I forgot," he said. He seemed vexed with himself.

Churchill's dinners were frequently rather trying to me. Personages of enormous importance used to drop in—and reveal themselves as rather asinine. At the best of times they sat dimly opposite to me, discomposed me, and disappeared. Sometimes they stared me down. That night there were two of them.

Gurnard I had heard of. One can't help hearing of a Chancellor of the Exchequer. The books of reference said that he was the son of one William Gurnard, Esq., of Grimsby; but I remember that once in my club a man who professed to know everything, assured me that W. Gurnard, Esq. (whom he had described as a fish salesman), was only an adoptive father. His rapid rise seemed to me inexplicable till the same man accounted for it with a shrug: "When a man of such ability believes in nothing, and sticks at nothing, there's no saying how far he may go. He has kicked away every ladder. He doesn't mean to come down."

This, no doubt, explained much; but not everything in his fabulous career. His adherents called him an inspired statesman; his enemies set him down a mere politician. He was a man of forty-five, thin, slightly bald, and with an icy assurance of manner. He was indifferent to attacks upon his character, but crushed mercilessly everyone who menaced his position. He stood alone, and a little mysterious; his own party was afraid of him.

Gurnard was quite hidden from me by table ornaments; the Duc de Mersch glowed with light and talked voluminously, as if he had for years and years been starved of human society. He glowed all over, it seemed to me. He had a glorious beard, that let one see very little of his florid face and took the edge away from an almost non-existent forehead and depressingly wrinkled eyelids. He spoke excellent English, rather slowly, as if he were forever replying to toasts to his health. It struck me that he seemed to treat Churchill in nuances as an inferior, whilst for the invisible Gurnard, he reserved an attitude of nervous self-assertion. He had apparently come to dilate on the *Système Groënlandais*, and he dilated. Some mistaken persons had insinuated that the *Système* was neither more nor less than a corporate exploitation of unhappy Esquimaux. De Mersch emphatically declared that those *mistaken* people were *mistaken*, declared it with official finality. The Esquimaux were not unhappy. I paid attention to my dinner, and let the discourse on the affairs of the Hyperborean Protectorate lapse into an unheeded murmur. I tried to be the simple amanuensis at the feast.

Suddenly, however, it struck me that de Mersch was talking at me; that he had by the merest shade raised his intonation.   He was dilating upon the immense international value of the proposed Trans-Greenland Railway.   Its importance to British trade was indisputable; even the opposition had no serious arguments to offer.   It was the obvious duty of the British Government to give the financial guarantee.   He would not insist upon the moral aspect of the work—it was unnecessary.   Progress, improvement, civilisation, a little less evil in the world—more light!   It was our duty not to count the cost of humanising a lower race.   Besides, the thing would pay like another Suez Canal.   Its terminus and the British coaling station would be on the west coast of the island.   .   .   .   I knew the man was talking at me—I wondered why.

Suddenly he turned his glowing countenance full upon me.

"I think I must have met a member of your family," he said.   The solution occurred to me.   I was a journalist, he a person interested in a railway that he wished the Government to back in some way or another.   His attempts to capture my suffrage no longer astonished me.   I murmured:

"Indeed!"

"In Paris—Mrs. Etchingham Granger," he said.

I said, "Oh, yes."

Miss Churchill came to the rescue.

"The Duc de Mersch means our friend, your aunt," she explained.   I had an unpleasant sensation.   Through fronds of asparagus fern I caught the eyes of Gurnard fixed upon me as though something had drawn his attention.   I returned his glance, tried to make his face out.   It had nothing distinctive in its half-hidden pallid oval; nothing that one could seize upon.   But it gave the impression of never having seen the light of day, of never having had the sun upon it. But the conviction that I had aroused his attention disturbed me. What could the man know about me? I seemed to feel his glance bore through the irises of my eyes into the back of my skull. The feeling was almost physical; it was as if some incredibly concentrant reflector had been turned upon me. Then the eyelids dropped over the metallic rings beneath them. Miss Churchill continued to explain.

"She has started a sort of *Salon des Causes Perdues* in the Faubourg Saint Germain." She was recording the vagaries of my aunt. The Duc laughed.

"Ah, yes," he said, "what a menagerie— Carlists, and Orleanists, and Papal Blacks. I wonder she has not held a bazaar in favour of your White Rose League."

"Ah, yes," I echoed, "I have heard that she was mad about the divine right of kings."

Miss Churchill rose, as ladies rise at the end of a dinner. I followed her out of the room, in obedience to some minute signal.

We were on the best of terms—we two. She mothered me, as she mothered everybody not beneath contempt or above a certain age. I liked her immensely— the masterful, absorbed, brown lady. As she walked up the stairs, she said, in half apology for withdrawing me.

"They've got things to talk about."

"Why, yes," I answered; "I suppose the railway matter has to be settled." She looked at me fixedly.

"You—you mustn't talk," she warned.

"Oh," I answered, "I'm not indiscreet—not essentially."

The other three were somewhat tardy in making their drawing-room appearance. I had a sense of them, leaning their heads together over the edges of the table. In the interim a rather fierce political dowager convoyed two well-controlled, blond daughters into the room. There was a continual coming and going of such people in the house; they did with Miss Churchill social business of some kind, arranged electoral rarée-shows, and what not; troubled me very little. On this occasion the blond daughters were types of the sixties' survivals—the type that unemotionally inspected albums. I was convoying them through a volume of views of Switzerland, the dowager was saying to Miss Churchill:

"You think, then, it will be enough if we have . . ." when the door opened behind my back. I looked round negligently and hastily returned to the consideration of a shining photograph of the Dent du Midi. A very gracious figure of a girl was embracing the grim Miss Churchill, as a gracious girl should virginally salute a grim veteran.

"Ah, my dear Miss Churchill!" a fluting voice filled the large room, "we were very nearly going back to Paris without once coming to see you. We are only over for two days—for the Tenants' Ball, and so my aunt . . . but surely that is Arthur. . . ."

I turned eagerly. It was the Dimensionist girl. She continued talking to Miss Churchill. "We meet so seldom, and we are never upon terms," she said lightly. "I assure you we are like cat and dog." She came toward me and the blond maidens disappeared, everybody, everything disappeared. I had not seen her for nearly a year. I had vaguely gathered from Miss Churchill that she was regarded as a sister of mine, that she had, with wealth inherited from a semi-fabulous Australian uncle, revived the glories of my aunt's house. I had never denied it, because I did not want to interfere with my aunt's attempts to regain some of the family's prosperity. It even had my sympathy to a small extent, for, after all, the family was my family too.

As a memory my pseudo-sister had been something bright and clear-cut and rather small; seen now, she was something that one could not look at for glow. She moved toward me, smiling and radiant, as a ship moves beneath towers of shining canvas. I was simply overwhelmed. I don't know what she said, what I said, what she did or I. I have an idea that we conversed for some minutes. I remember that she said, at some point,

"Go away now; I want to talk to Mr. Gurnard."

As a matter of fact, Gurnard was making toward her —a deliberate, slow progress. She greeted him with nonchalance, as, beneath eyes, a woman greets a man she knows intimately. I found myself hating him, thinking that he was not the sort of man she ought to know.

"It's settled?" she asked him, as he came within range. He looked at me inquiringly—insolently. She said, "My brother," and he answered:

"Oh, yes," as I moved away. I hated the man and I could not keep my eyes off him and her. I went and stood against the mantel-piece. The Duc de Mersch bore down upon them, and I welcomed his interruption until I saw that he, too, was intimate with her, intimate with a pomposity of flourishes as irritating as Gurnard's nonchalance.

I stood there and glowered at them. I noted her excessive beauty; her almost perilous self-possession while she stood talking to those two men. Of me there was nothing left but the eyes. I had no mind, no thoughts. I saw the three figures go through the attitudes of conversation—she very animated, de Mersch

grotesquely *empressé*, Gurnard undisguisedly saturnine.
He repelled me exactly as grossly vulgar men had the
power of doing, but he, himself, was not that—there was
something . . . something. I could not quite
make out his face, I never could. I never did, any
more than I could ever quite visualise hers. I wondered vaguely how Churchill could work in harness with
such a man, how he could bring himself to be closeted,
as he had just been, with him and with a fool like de
Mersch—I should have been afraid.

As for de Mersch, standing between those two, he
seemed like a country lout between confederate sharpers.
It struck me that she let me see, made me see, that
she and Gurnard had an understanding, made manifest
to me by glances that passed when the Duc had his un-
observant eyes turned elsewhere.

I saw Churchill, in turn, move desultorily toward
them, drawn in, like a straw toward a little whirlpool.
I turned my back in a fury of jealousy.

CHAPTER NINE

I HAD a pretty bad night after that, and was not much in the mood for Fox on the morrow. The sight of her had dwarfed everything; the thought of her disgusted me with everything, made me out of conceit with the world—with that part of the world that had become my world. I wanted to get up into hers—and I could not see any way. The room in which Fox sat seemed to be hopelessly off the road—to be hopelessly off any road to any place; to be the end of a blind alley. One day I might hope to occupy such a room—in my shirt-sleeves, like Fox. But that was not the end of my career—not the end that I desired. She had upset me.

"You've just missed Polehampton," Fox said; "wanted to get hold of your 'Atmospheres.'"

"Oh, damn Polehampton," I said, "and particularly damn the 'Atmospheres.'"

"Willingly," Fox said, "but I told Mr. P. that you were willing if . . ."

"I don't want to know," I repeated. "I tell you I'm sick of the things."

"Want a change," he asserted sympathetically, "I *thought* you would."

It struck me as disgusting that a person like Fox should think about me at all. "Oh, I'll see it through," I said. "Who's the next?"

"We've got to have the Duc de Mersch now," he answered, "De Mersch as State Founder—written as large as you can—all across the page. The moment's come and we've got to rope it in, that's all. I've been middling good to you . . . You understand . . ."

He began to explain in his dark sentences. The time had come for an energetically engineered boom in de Mersch—a boom all along the line. And I was to commence the campaign. Fox had been good to me and I was to repay him. I listened in a sort of apathetic indifference.

"Oh, very well," I said. I was subconsciously aware that, as far as I was concerned, the determining factor of the situation was the announcement that de Mersch was to be in Paris. If he had been in his own particular grand duchy I wouldn't have gone after him. For a moment I thought of the interview as taking place in London. But Fox—ostensibly, at least—wasn't even aware of de Mersch's visit; spoke of him as being in Paris— in a flat in which he was accustomed to interview the continental financiers who took up so much of his time.

I realised that I wanted to go to Paris because she was there. She had said that she was going to Paris on the morrow of yesterday. The name was pleasant to me, and it turned the scale.

Fox's eyes remained upon my face.

"Do you good, eh?" he dimly interpreted my thoughts. "A run over. I thought you'd like it and, look here, Polehampton's taken over the *Bi-Monthly;* wants to get new blood into it, see? He'd take something. I've been talking to him —a short series. . . . 'Aspects.' That sort of thing." I tried to work myself into some sort of enthusiasm of gratitude. I knew that Fox had spoken well of me to Polehampton—as a sort of set off.

"You go and see Mr. P.," he confirmed; "it's really all arranged. And then get off to Paris as fast as you can and have a good time."

"Have I been unusually cranky lately?" I asked.

"Oh, you've been a little off the hooks, I thought, for the last week or so."

He took up a large bottle of white mucilage, and I accepted it as a sign of dismissal. I was touched by his solicitude for my health. It always did touch me, and I found myself unusually broad-minded in thought as I went down the terra-cotta front steps into the streets. For all his frank vulgarity, for all his shirt-sleeves—I somehow regarded that habit of his as the final mark of the Beast—and the Louis Quinze accessories, I felt a warm good-feeling for the little man.

I made haste to see Polehampton, to beard him in a sort of den that contained a number of shelves of books selected for their glittering back decoration. They gave the impression that Mr. Polehampton wished to suggest to his visitors the fitness and propriety of clothing their walls with the same gilt cloth. They gave that idea, but I think that, actually, Mr. Polehampton took an æsthetic delight in the gilding. He was not a publisher by nature. He had drifted into the trade and success, but beneath a polish of acquaintance retained a fine awe for a book as such. In early life he had had such shining things on a shiny table in a parlour. He had a similar awe for his daughter, who had been born after his entry into the trade, and who had the literary flavour —a flavour so pronounced that he dragged her by the heels into any conversation with us who hewed his raw material, expecting, I suppose, to cow us. For the greater good of this young lady he had bought the *Bi-Monthly*—one of the portentous political organs. He had, they said, ideas of forcing a seat out of the party as a recompense.

It didn't matter much what was the nature of my series of articles. I was to get the atmosphere of cities as I had got those of the various individuals. I seemed to pay on those lines, and Miss Polehampton commended me.

"My daughter likes . . . eh . . . your touch, you know, and . . ." His terms were decent —for the man, and were offered with a flourish that indicated special benevolence and a reference to the hundred pounds. I was at a loss to account for his manner until he began to stammer out an indication. Its lines were that I knew Fox, and I knew Churchill and the Duc de Mersch, and the *Hour*. "And those financial articles . . . in the *Hour* . . . were they now? . . . *Were* they . . . was the Trans-Greenland railway actually . . . did I think it would be worth one's while . . . in fact . . ." and so on.

I never was any good in a situation of that sort, never any good at all. I ought to have assumed blank ignorance, but the man's eyes pleaded; it seemed a tremendous matter to him. I tried to be non-committal, and said: "Of course I haven't any right." But I had a vague, stupid sense that loyalty to Churchill demanded that I should back up a man he was backing. As a matter of fact, nothing so direct was a-gate, it couldn't have been. It was something about shares in one of de Mersch's other enterprises. Polehampton was going to pick them up for nothing, and they were going to rise when the boom in de Mersch's began—something of the sort. And the boom would begin as soon as the news of the agreement about the railway got abroad.

I let him get it out of me in a way that makes the thought of that bare place with its gilt book-backs and its three uncomfortable office-chairs and the ground-glass windows through which one read the inversion of the legend "Polehampton," all its gloom and its rigid

lines and its pallid light, a memory of confusion. And
Polehampton was properly grateful, and invited me to
dine with him and his phantasmal daughter—who
wanted to make my acquaintance. It was like a command to a state banquet given by a palace official, and
Lea would be invited to meet me. Miss Polehampton
did not like Lea, but he had to be asked once a year—
to encourage good feeling, I suppose. The interview
dribbled out on those lines. I asked if it was one of
Lea's days at the office. It was not. I tried to put in
a good word for Lea, but it was not very effective.
Polehampton was too subject to his assistant's thorns to
be responsive to praise of him.

So I hurried out of the place. I wanted to be out of
this medium in which my ineffectiveness threatened to
proclaim itself to me. It was not a very difficult matter. I had, in those days, rooms in one of the political
journalists' clubs—a vast mausoleum of white tiles.
But a man used to pack my portmanteau very efficiently
and at short notice. At the station one of those coincidences that are not coincidences made me run against
the great Callan. He was rather unhappy—found it
impossible to make an already distracted porter listen
to the end of one of his sentences with two-second waits
between each word. For that reason he brightened to
see me—was delighted to find a through-journey companion who would take him on terms of greatness. In
the railway carriage, divested of troublesome bags that
imparted anxiety to his small face and a stagger to his
walk, he swelled to his normal dimensions.

"So you're—going to—Paris," he meditated, "for the
Hour."

"I'm going to Paris for the *Hour*," I agreed.

"Ah!" he went on, "you're going to interview the
Elective Grand Duke . . ."

"We call him the Duc de Mersch," I interrupted flippantly. It was a matter of nuances. The Elective
Grand Duke was a philanthropist and a State Founder,
the Duc de Mersch was the hero as financier.

"Of Holstein-Launewitz," Callan ignored. The title
slipped over his tongue like the last drops of some in-
estimable oily vintage.

"I might have saved you the trouble. I'm going to
see him myself."

"*You*," I italicised. It struck me as phenomenal
and rather absurd that everybody that I came across
should, in some way or other, be mixed up with this portentous philanthropist. It was as if a fisherman were
drawing in a ground line baited with hundreds of hooks.
He had a little offended air.

"He, or, I should say, a number of people interested
in a philanthropic society, have asked me to go to
Greenland."

"Do they want to get rid of you?" I asked, flippantly.
I was made to know my place.

"My dear fellow," Callan said, in his most deliberate,
most Olympian tone. "I believe you're entirely mistaken. I believe . . . I've been informed that the
Système Groënlandais is one of the healthiest places in
the Polar regions. There are interested persons
who . . ."

"So I've heard," I interrupted, "but I can assure you
I've heard nothing but good of the Système and the
. . . and its philanthropists. I meant nothing
against them. I was only astonished that you should
go to such a place."

"I have been asked to go upon a mission," he explained, seriously, "to ascertain what the truth about
the Système really is. It is a new country with, I am
assured, a great future in store. A great deal of English

money has been invested in its securities, and naturally great interest is taken in its affairs."

"So it seems," I said, "I seem to run upon it at every hour of the day and night."

"Ah, yes," Callan rhapsodised, "it has a great future in store, a great future. The Duke is a true philanthropist. He has taken infinite pains—infinite pains. He wished to build up a model state, *the* model protectorate of the world, a place where perfect equality shall obtain for all races, all creeds, and all colours. You would scarcely believe how he has worked to ensure the happiness of the native races. He founded the great society to protect the Esquimaux, the Society for the Regeneration of the Arctic Regions— the S.R.A.R. —as you called it, and now he is only waiting to accomplish his greatest project—the Trans-Greenland railway. When that is done, he will hand over the Système to his own people. That is the act of a great man."

"Ah, yes," I said.

"Well," Callan began again, but suddenly paused. "By-the-bye, this must go no farther," he said, anxiously, "I will let you have full particulars when the time is ripe."

"My dear Callan," I said, touchily, "I can hold my tongue."

He went off at tangent.

"I don't want you to take my word—I haven't seen it yet. But I feel assured about it myself. The most distinguished people have spoken to me in its favour. The celebrated traveller, Aston, spoke of it with tears in his eyes. He was the first governor-general, you know. Of course I should not take any interest in it, if I were not satisfied as to that. It is precisely because I feel that the thing is one of the finest monuments of a grand century that I am going to lend it the weight of my pen."

"I quite understand," I assured him; then, solicitously, "I hope they don't expect you to do it for nothing."

"Oh, dear, no," Callan answered.

"Ah, well, I wish you luck," I said. "They couldn't have got a better man to win over the National conscience. I suppose it comes to that."

Callan nodded.

"I fancy I have the ear of the public," he said. He seemed to get satisfaction from the thought.

The train entered Folkestone Harbour. The smell of the sea and the easy send of the boat put a little heart into me, but my spirits were on the down grade. Callan was a trying companion. The sight of him stirred uneasy emotions, the sound of his voice jarred.

"Are you coming to the Grand?" he said, as we passed St. Denis.

"My God, no," I answered, hotly, "I'm going across the river."

"Ah," he murmured, "the Quartier Latin. I wish I could come with you. But I've my reputation to think of. You'd be surprised how people get to hear of my movements. Besides, I'm a family man."

I was agitatedly silent. The train steamed into the glare of the electric lights, and, getting into a fiacre, I breathed again. I seemed to be at the entrance of a new life, a better sort of paradise, during that drive across the night city. (In London one is always a passenger, in Paris one has reached a goal.) The crowds on the pavements, under the plane-trees, in the black shadows, in the white glare of the open spaces, are at leisure—they go nowhere, seek nothing beyond.

We crossed the river, the unwinking towers of Notre Dame towering pallidly against the dark sky behind us; rattled into the new light of the resuming boulevard;

turned up a dark street, and came to a halt before a half-familiar shut door. You know how one wakes the sleepy concierge, how one takes one's candle, climbs up hundreds and hundreds of smooth stairs, following the slip-shod footfalls of a half-awakened guide upward through Rembrandt's own shadows, and how one's final sleep is sweetened by the little inconveniences of a strange bare room and of a strange hard bed.

CHAPTER TEN

BEFORE noon of the next day I was ascending the stairs of the new house in which the Duc had his hermitage. There was an air of secrecy in the broad publicity of the carpeted stairs that led to his flat; a hush in the atmosphere; in the street itself, a glorified *cul de sac* that ran into the bustling life of the Italiens. It had the sudden sluggishness of a back-water. One seemed to have grown suddenly deaf in the midst of the rattle.

There was an incredible suggestion of silence—the silence of a private detective—in the mien of the servant who ushered me into a room. He was the English servant of the theatre—the English servant that foreigners affect. The room had a splendour of its own, not a cheaply vulgar splendour, but the vulgarity of the most lavish plush and purple kind. The air was heavy, killed by the scent of exotic flowers, darkened by curtains that suggested the voluminous velvet backgrounds of certain old portraits. The Duc de Mersch had carried with him into this place of retirement the taste of the New Palace, that show-place of his that was the stupefaction of swarms of honest tourists.

I remembered soon enough that the man was a philanthropist, that he might be an excellent man of heart and indifferent of taste. He must be. But I was prone to be influenced by things of this sort, and felt depressed at the thought that so much of royal excellence should weigh so heavily in the wrong scale of the balance of the applied arts. I turned my back on the room and gazed at the blazing white decorations of the opposite house-fronts.

A door behind me must have opened, for I heard the sounds of a concluding tirade in a high-pitched voice.

"*Et quant à un duc de farce, je ne m'en fiche pas mal, moi,*" it said in an accent curiously compounded of the foreign and the *coulisse.* A muttered male remonstrance ensued, and then, with disconcerting clearness:

"*Gr-r-rangeur—Eschingan—eh bien—il entend. Et moi, j'entends, moi aussi. Tu veux me jouer contre elle. La Grangeur—pah! Consoles-toi avec elle, mon vieux. Je ne veux plus de toi. Tu m'as donné de tes sales rentes Groënlandoises, et je n'ai pas pu les vendre. Ah, vieux farceur, tu vas voir ce que j'en vais faire.*"

A glorious creature—a really glorious creature—came out of an adjoining room. She was as frail, as swaying as a garden lily. Her great blue eyes turned irefully upon me, her bowed lips parted, her nostrils quivered.

"*Et quant à vous, M. Grangeur Eschingan,*" she began, "*je vais vous donner mon idée à moi . . .*"

I did not understand the situation in the least, but I appreciated the awkwardness of it. The world seemed to be standing on its head. I was overcome; but I felt for the person in the next room. I did not know what to do. Suddenly I found myself saying:

"I am extremely sorry, madam, but I don't understand French." An expression of more intense vexation passed into her face—her beautiful face. I fancy she wished—wished intensely—to give me the benefit of her "*idée à elle.*" She made a quick, violent gesture of disgusted contempt, and turned toward the half-open door from which she had come. She began again to dilate upon the little weaknesses of the person behind, when silently and swiftly it closed. We heard the lock click. With extraordinary quickness she had her mouth at the keyhole: "*Peeg, peeg,*" she enunciated. Then she stood to her full height, her face became calm, her manner stately. She glided half way across the room, paused, looked at me, and pointed toward the unmoving door.

"*Peeg, peeg,*" she explained, mysteriously. I think she was warning me against the wiles of the person behind the door. I gazed into her great eyes. "I understand," I said, gravely. She glided from the room. For me the incident supplied a welcome touch of comedy. I had leisure for thought. The door remained closed. It made the Duc a more real person for me. I had regarded him as a rather tiresome person in whom a pompous philanthropism took the place of human feelings. It amused me to be called *Le Grangeur*. It amused me, and I stood in need of amusement. Without it I might never have written the article on the Duc. I had started out that morning in a state of nervous irritation. I had wanted more than ever to have done with the thing, with the *Hour*, with journalism, with everything. But this little new experience buoyed me up, set my mind working in less morbid lines. I began to wonder whether de Mersch would funk, or whether he would take my non-comprehension of the woman's tirades as a thing assured.

The door at which I had entered, by which she had left, opened.

He must have impressed me in some way or other that evening at the Churchills. He seemed a very stereotyped image in my memory. He spoke just as he had spoken, moved his hands just as I expected him to move them. He called for no modification of my views of his person. (As a rule one classes a man so-and-so at first meeting, modifies the classification at each subsequent one, and so on.) He seemed to be all affability, of an adipose turn. He had the air of the man of the world among men of the world; but none of the unconscious reserve of manner that one expects to find in the temporarily great. He had in its place a kind of sub-sulkiness, as if he regretted the pedestal from which he had descended.

In his slow commercial English he apologised for having kept me waiting; he had been taking the air of this fine morning, he said. He mumbled the words with his eyes on my waistcoat, with an air that accorded rather ill with the semblance of portentous probity that his beard conferred on him. But he set an eye-glass in his left eye immediately afterward, and looked straight at me as if in challenge. With a smiling "Don't mention it," I tried to demonstrate that I met him halfway.

"You want to interview me," he said blandly. "I am only too pleased. I suppose it is about my Arctic schemes that you wish to know. I will do what I can to inform you. You perhaps remember what I said when I had the pleasure of meeting you at the house of the Right Honourable Mr. Churchill. It has been the dream of my life to leave behind me a happy and contented State—as much as laws and organisation can make one. This is what I should most like the English to know of me." He was a dull talker. I supposed that philanthropists and state founders kept their best faculties for their higher pursuits. I imagined the low, receding forehead and the pink-nailed, fleshy hands to belong to a new Solon, a latter-day Æneas. I tried to work myself into the properly enthusiastic frame of mind. After all, it was a great work that he had undertaken. I was too much given to dwell upon intellectual gifts. These the Duc seemed to lack. I credited him with having let them be merged in his one noble idea.

He furnished me with statistics. They had laid down

so many miles of railways, used so many engines of British construction. They had taught the natives to use and to value sewing-machines and European costumes. So many hundred of English younger sons had gone to make their fortunes and, incidentally, to enlighten the Esquimaux—so many hundreds of French, of Germans, Greeks, Russians. All these lived and moved in harmony, employed, happy, free labourers, protected by the most rigid laws. Man-eating, fetich-worship, slavery had been abolished, stamped out. The great international society for the preservation of Polar freedom watched over all, suggested new laws, modified the old. The country was unhealthy, but not to men of clean lives—*hominibus bonœ voluntatis*. It asked for no others.

"I have had to endure much misrepresentation. I have been called names," the Duc said.

The figure of the lady danced before my eyes, lithe, supple—a statue endued with the motion of a serpent. I seemed to see her sculptured white hand pointing to the closed door.

"Ah, yes,' I said, "but one knows the people **who** call you names."

"Well, then," he answered, "it is your task to make them know the truth. Your nation has so much power. If it will only realise."

"I will do my best," I said.

I saw the apotheosis of the Press—a Press that makes a State Founder suppliant to a man like myself. For he had the tone of a deprecating petitioner. I stood between himself and a people, the arbiter of the peoples, of the kings of the future. I was nothing, nobody; yet here I stood in communion with one of those who change the face of continents. He had need of me, of the power that was behind me. It was strange to be alone in that room with that man—to be there just as I might be in my own little room alone with any other man.

I was not unduly elated, you must understand. It was nothing to me. I was just a person elected by some suffrage of accidents. Even in my own eyes I was merely a symbol—the sign visible of incomprehensible power.

"I will do my best," I said.

"Ah, yes, do," he said, "Mr. Churchill told me how nicely you can do such things."

I said that it was very kind of Mr. Churchill. The tension of the conversation was relaxed. The Duc asked if I had yet seen my aunt.

"I had forgotten her," I said.

"Oh, you must see her," he said; "she is a most re-markable lady. She is one of my relaxations. All Paris talks about her, I can assure you."

"I had no idea," I said.

"Oh, cultivate her," he said; "you will be amused."

"I will," I said, as I took my leave.

I went straight home to my little room above the roofs. I began at once to write my article, working at high pressure, almost hysterically. I remember that place and that time so well. In moments of emotion one gazes fixedly at things, hardly conscious of them. Afterward one remembers.

I can still see the narrow room, the bare, brown, dis-coloured walls, the incongruous marble clock on the mantel-piece, the single rickety chair that swayed be-neath me. I could almost draw the tortuous pattern of the faded cloth that hid the round table at which I sat. The ink was thick, pale, and sticky; the pen spluttered. I wrote furiously, anxious to be done with it. Once I went and leaned over the balcony, trying to hit on a word that would not come. Miles down below, little people crawled over the cobbled street, little carts rattled, little workmen let down casks into a cellar. It was all very gray, small, and clear.

Through the open window of an opposite garret I could see a sculptor working at a colossal clay model. In his white blouse he seemed big, out of all proportion to the rest of the world. Level with my eyes there were flat lead roofs and chimneys. On one of these was scrawled, in big, irregular, blue-painted letters: "*A bas Coignet.*"

Great clouds began to loom into view over the housetops, rounded, toppling masses of gray, lit up with sullen orange against the pale limpid blue of the sky. I stood and looked at all these objects. I had come out here to think—thoughts had deserted me. I could only look.

The clouds moved imperceptibly, fatefully onward, a streak of lightning tore them apart. They whirled like tortured smoke and grew suddenly black. Large spots of rain with jagged edges began to fall on the lead floor of my balcony.

I turned into the twilight of my room and began to write. I can still feel the tearing of my pen-point on the coarse paper. It was a hindrance to thought, but my flow of words ignored it, gained impetus from it, as a stream does at the breaking of a dam.

I was writing a pæan to a great coloniser. That sort of thing was in the air then. I was drawn into it, carried away by my subject. Perhaps I let it do so because it was so little familiar to my lines of thought. It was fresh ground and I revelled in it. I committed myself to that kind of emotional, lyrical outburst that one dislikes so much on re-reading. I was half conscious of the fact, but I ignored it.

The thunderstorm was over, and there was a moist sparkling freshness in the air when I hurried with my copy to the *Hour* office in the Avenue de l'Opéra. I wished to be rid of it, to render impossible all chance of revision on the morrow.

I wanted, too, to feel elated; I expected it. It was a right. At the office I found the foreign correspondent, a little cosmopolitan Jew whose eyebrows began their growth on the bridge of his nose. He was effusive and familiar, as the rest of his kind.

"Hullo, Granger," was his greeting. I was used to regarding myself as fallen from a high estate, but I was not yet so humble in spirit as to relish being called Granger by a stranger of his stamp. I tried to freeze him politely.

"Read your stuff in the *Hour*," was his rejoinder; "jolly good I call it. Been doing old Red-Beard? Let's have a look. Yes, yes. That's the way—that's the real thing—I call it. Must have bored you to death . . . old de Mersch I mean. I ought to have had the job, you know. My business, interviewing people in Paris. But *I* don't mind. Much rather you did it than I. You do it a heap better."

I murmured thanks. There was a pathos about the sleek little man—a pathos that is always present in the type. He seemed to be trying to assume a deprecating equality.

"Where are you going to-night?" he asked, with sudden effusiveness. I was taken aback. One is not used to being asked these questions after five minutes' acquaintance. I said that I had no plans.

"Look here," he said, brightening up, "come and have dinner with me at Breguet's, and look in at the Opéra afterward. We'll have a real nice chat."

I was too tired to frame an adequate excuse. Besides, the little man was as eager as a child for a new toy. We went to Breguet's and had a really excellent dinner.

"Always come here," he said; "one meets a lot of swells. It runs away with a deal of money—but I don't care to do things on the cheap, not for the *Hour*, you know. You can always be certain when I say that I have a thing from a senator that he is a senator, and not an old woman in a paper kiosque. Most of them do that sort of thing, you know."

"I always wondered," I said, mildly.

"That's de Sourdam I nodded to as we came in, and that old chap there is Pluyvis—the Affaire man, you know. I must have a word with him in a minute, if you'll excuse me."

He began to ask affectionately after the health of the excellent Fox, asked if I saw him often, and so on and so on. I divined with amusement that was pleasurable that the little man had his own little axe to grind, and thought I might take a turn at the grindstone if he managed me well. So he nodded to de Sourdam of the Austrian embassy and had his word with Pluyvis, and rejoiced to have impressed me—I could see him bubble with happiness and purr. He proposed that we should stroll as far as the paper kiosque that he patronised habitually—it was kept by a fellow-Israelite—a snuffy little old woman.

I understood that in the joy of his heart he was for expanding, for wasting a few minutes on a stroll.

"Haven't stretched my legs for months," he explained.

We strolled there through the summer twilight. It was so pleasant to saunter through the young summer night. There were so many little things to catch the eyes, so many of the little things down near the earth; expressions on faces of the passers, the set of a collar, the quaint foreign tightness of waist of a good bourgeoise who walked arm in arm with her perspiring spouse.

The gilding on the statue of Joan of Arc had a pleasant littleness of Philistinism, the arcades of the Rue de Rivoli broke up the gray light pleasantly too. I remembered a little shop—a little Greek affair with a windowful of pinchbeck—where I had been given a false five-franc piece years and years ago. The same villainous old Levantine stood in the doorway, perhaps the fez that he wore was the same fez. The little old woman that we strolled to was bent nearly double. Her nose touched her wares as often as not, her mittened hands sought quiveringly the papers that the correspondent asked for. I liked him the better for his solicitude for this forlorn piece of flotsam of his own race.

"Always come here," he exclaimed; "one gets into habits. Very honest woman, too; you can be certain of getting your change. If you're a stranger you can't be sure that they won't give you Italian silver, you know."

"Oh, I know," I answered. I knew, too, that he wished me to purchase something. I followed the course of her groping hands, caught sight of the *Revue Rouge*, and remembered that it contained something about Greenland. I helped myself to it, paid for it, and received my just change. I felt that I had satisfied the little man, and felt satisfied with myself.

"I want to see Radet's article on Greenland," I said.

"Oh, yes," he explained, once more exhibiting himself in the capacity of the man who knows, "Radet gives it to them. Rather a lark, I call it, though you mustn't let old de Mersch know you read him. Radet got sick of Cochin, and tried Greenland. He's getting touched by the Whites, you know. They say that the priests don't like the way the Système's playing into the hands of the Protestants and the English Government. So they set Radet on to write it down. He's going in for mysticism and all that sort of thing—just like all these French jokers are doing. Got deuced thick with that lot in the F. St. Germain—some relation of yours, ain't they? Rather a lark that lot, quite the thing just now, everyone goes there; old de Mersch too. Have frightful rows sometimes, such a mixed lot, you see." The good little man rattled amiably along beside me.

"Seems quite funny to be buying books," he said. "I haven't read a thing I've bought, not for years."

We reached the Opéra in time for the end of the first act—it was Aïda, I think. My little friend had a free pass all over the house. I had not been in it for years. In the old days I had always seen the stage from a great height, craning over people's heads in a sultry twilight; now I saw it on a level, seated at my ease. I had only the power of the Press to thank for the change.

"Come here as often as I can," my companion said: "can't do without music when it's to be had." Indeed he had the love of his race for it. It seemed to soften him, to change his nature, as he sat silent by my side.

But the closing notes of each scene found him out in the cool of the corridors, talking, and being talked to by any one that would vouchsafe him a word.

"Pick up a lot here," he explained.

After the finale we leaned over one of the side balconies to watch the crowd streaming down the marble staircases. It is a scene that I never tire of. There is something so fantastically tawdry in the coloured marble of the architecture. It is for all the world like a triumph of ornamental soap work; one expects to smell the odours. And the torrent of humanity pouring liquidly aslant through the mirror-like light, and the spaciousness . . . Yes, it is fantastic, somehow; ironical, too.

I was watching the devious passage of a rather drunken, gigantic, florid Englishman, wondering, I think, how he would reach his bed.

"That must be a relation of yours," the correspondent said, pointing. My glance followed the line indicated by his pale finger. I made out the glorious beard of the Duc de Mersch; on his arm was an old lady to whom he seemed to pay deferential attention. His head was bent on one side; he was smiling frankly. A little behind them, on the stairway, there was a space. Perhaps I was mistaken; perhaps there was no space—I don't know. I was only conscious of a figure, an indescribably clear-cut woman's figure, gliding down the way. It had a coldness, a self-possession, a motion of its own. In that clear, transparent, shimmering light, every little fold of the dress, every little shadow of the white arms, the white shoulders, came up to me. The face turned up to meet mine. I remember so well the light shining down on the face, not a shadow anywhere, not a shadow beneath the eyebrows, the nostrils, the waves of hair. It was a vision of light, threatening, sinister.

She smiled, her lips parted.

"You come to me to-morrow," she said. Did I hear the words, did her lips merely form them? She was far, far down below me; the air was alive with the rustling of feet, of garments, of laughter, full of sounds that made themselves heard, full of sounds that would not be caught.

"You come to me . . . to-morrow."

The old lady on the Duc de Mersch's arm was obviously my aunt. I did not see why I should not go to them to-morrow. It struck me suddenly and rather pleasantly that this was, after all, my family. This old lady actually was a connection more close than any one else in the world. As for the girl, to all intents and, in everyone else's eyes, she was my sister. I cannot say I disliked having her for my sister, either. I stood looking down upon them and felt less alone than I had done for many years.

A minute scuffle of the shortest duration was taking place beside me. There were a couple of men at my elbow. I don't in the least know what they were—perhaps marquises, perhaps railway employees—one never can tell over there. One of them was tall and blond, with a heavy, bow-shaped red moustache—Irish in type; the other of no particular height, excellently groomed, dark, and exemplary. I knew he was exemplary from some detail of costume that I can't remember—his gloves or a strip of silk down the sides of his trousers—something of the sort. The blond was saying something that I did not catch. I heard the words "de Mersch" and "*Anglaise*," and saw the dark man turn his attention to the little group below. Then I caught my own name mispronounced and somewhat of a stumbling-block to a high-pitched contemptuous intonation. The little correspondent, who was on my other arm, started visibly and moved swiftly behind my back.

"*Messieurs*," he said in an urgent whisper, and drew them to a little distance. I saw him say something, saw them pivot to look at me, shrug their shoulders and walk away. I didn't in the least grasp the significance of the scene—not then.

"What's the matter?" I asked my returning friend; "were they talking about me?" He answered nervously.

"Oh, it was about your aunt's Salon, you know. They might have been going to say something awkward . . one never knows."

"They really *do* talk about it then?" I said. "I've a good mind to attend one of their exhibitions."

"Why, of course," he said, "you ought. I really think you *ought*."

"I'll go to-morrow," I answered.

CHAPTER ELEVEN

I COULDN'T get to sleep that night, but lay and tossed, lit my candle and read, and so on, forever and ever—for an eternity. I was confoundedly excited; there were a hundred things to be thought about; clamouring to be thought about; out-clamouring the recurrent chimes of some near clock. I began to read the article by Radet in the *Revue Rouge*—the one I had bought of the old woman in the kiosque. It upset me a good deal— that article. It gave away the whole Greenland show so completely that the ecstatic bosh I had just des- patched to the *Hour* seemed impossible. I suppose the good Radet had his axe to grind—just as I had had to grind the State Founder's, but Radet's axe didn't show. I was reading about an inland valley, a broad, shadowy, gray thing; immensely broad, immensely shadowy, winding away between immense, half-invisible moun- tains into the silence of an unknown country. A little band of men, microscopic figures in that immensity, in those mists, crept slowly up it. A man among them was speaking; I seemed to hear his voice, low, monoto- nous, overpowered by the wan light and the silence and the vastness.

And how well it was done—how the man could write; how skilfully he made his points. There was no slosh about it, no sentiment. The touch was light, in places even gay. He saw so well the romance of that dun band that had cast remorse behind; that had no return, no future, that spread desolation desolately. This was merely a review article—a thing that in England would have been unreadable; the narrative of a nomad of some genius. I could never have written like that—I should have spoilt it somehow. It set me tingling with desire, with the desire that transcends the sexual; the desire for the fine phrase, for the right word—for all the other intangibles. And I had been wasting all this time; had been writing my inanities. I must go away; must get back, right back to the old road, must work. There was so little time. It was unpleasant, too, to have been mixed up in this affair, to have been trepanned into doing my best to help it on its foul way. God knows I had little of the humanitarian in me. If people must murder in the by-ways of an immense world, they must do murder and pay the price. But that I should have been mixed up in such was not what I had wanted. I must have done with it all; with all this sort of thing, must get back to my old self, must get back. I seemed to hear the slow words of the Duc de Mersch.

"We have increased the exports by so much; the imports by so much. We have protected the natives, have kept their higher interests ever present in our minds. And through it all we have never forgotten the mission entrusted to us by Europe—to remove the evil of darkness from the earth—to root out barbarism with its nameless horrors, whose existence has been a blot on our consciences. Men of good-will and self-sacrifice are doing it now—are laying down their priceless lives to root out . . . to root out . . ."

Of course they *were* rooting them out.

It didn't very much matter to me. One supposes that that sort of native exists for that sort of thing—to be rooted out by men of good-will, with careers to make. The point was that that was what they were really doing out there—rooting out the barbarians as well as the barbarism, and proving themselves worthy of their hire.

And I had been writing them up and was no better than the farcical governor of a department who would write on the morrow to protest that that was what they did not do. You see I had a sort of personal pride in those days; and preferred to think of myself as a decent person. I knew that people would say the same sort of thing about me that they said about all the rest of them. I couldn't very well protest. I *had* been scratching the backs of all sorts of creatures; out of friendship, out of love—for all sorts of reasons. This was only a sort of last straw—or perhaps it was the sight of her that had been the last straw. It seemed naïvely futile to have been wasting my time over Mrs. Hartly and those she stood for, when there was something so different in the world—something so like a current of east wind.

That vein of thought kept me awake, and a worse came to keep it company. The men from the next room came home—students, I suppose. They talked gaily enough, their remarks interspersed by the thuds of falling boots and the other incomprehensible noises of the night. Through the flimsy partition I caught half sentences in that sort of French intonation that is so impossible to attain. It reminded me of the voices of the two men at the Opéra. I began to wonder what they had been saying—what they could have been saying that concerned me and affected the little correspondent to interfere. Suddenly the thing dawned upon me with the startling clearness of a figure in a complicated pattern—a clearness from which one cannot take one's eyes.

It threw everything—the whole world—into more unpleasant relations with me than even the Greenland affair. They had not been talking about my aunt and her Salon, but about my . . . my sister. She was de Mersch's "*Anglaise*." I did not believe it, but probably all Paris—the whole world—said she was. And to the whole world I was her brother! Those two men who had looked at me over their shoulders had shrugged and said, "Oh, *he's* . . ." And the whole world wherever I went would whisper in asides, "Don't you know Granger? He's the brother. De Mersch employs him."

I began to understand everything; the woman in de Mersch's room with her "Eschingan-Grangeur-r-r"; the deference of the little Jew—the man who knew. *He* knew that I—that I, who patronised him, was a person to stand well with because of my—my sister's hold over de Mersch. I wasn't, of course, but you can't understand how the whole thing maddened me all the same. I hated the world—this world of people who whispered and were whispered to, of men who knew and men who wanted to know—the shadowy world of people who didn't matter, but whose eyes and voices were all round one and did somehow matter. I knew well enough how it had come about. It was de Mersch —the State Founder, with his shamed face and his pallid hands. She had been attracted by his air of greatness, by his elective grand-dukedom, by his pro-testations. Women are like that. She had been at-tracted and didn't know what she was doing, didn't know what the world was over here—how people talked. She had been excited by the whirl and flutter of it, and perhaps she didn't care. The thing must come to an end, however. She had said that I should go to her on the morrow. Well, I would go, and I would put a stop to this. I had suddenly discovered how very much I was a Granger of Etchingham, after all I *had* family traditions and graves behind me. And for the sake of all these people whose one achievement had been the making of a good name I *had* to intervene now. After all—"*Bon sang ne*"—does not get itself talked about in *that* way.

The early afternoon of the morrow found me in a great

room—a faded, sombre salon of the house my aunt had taken in the Faubourg Saint Germain. Numbers of strong-featured people were talking in groups among the tables and chairs of a time before the Revolution. I rather forget how I had got there, and what had gone before. I must have arisen late and passed the intervening hours in a state of trepidation. I was going to see her, and I was like a cub in love, with a man's place to fill. It was a preposterous state of things that set the solid world in a whirl. Once there, my eyes suddenly took in things.

I had a sense of her standing by my side. She had just introduced me to my aunt—a heavy-featured, tired-eyed village tyrant. She was so obviously worn out, so obviously "not what she had been," that her face would have been pitiful but for its immovable expression of class pride. The Grangers of Etchingham, you see, were so absolutely at the top of their own particular kind of tree that it was impossible for them to meet any one who was not an inferior. A man might be a cabinet minister, might even be a prince, but he couldn't be a Granger of Etchingham, couldn't have such an assortment of graves, each containing a Granger, behind his back. The expression didn't even lift for me who had. It couldn't, it was fixed there. One wondered what she was doing in this *galère*. It seemed impossible that she should interest herself in the restoration of the Bourbons—they were all very well, but they weren't even English, let alone a county family. I figured it out that she must have set her own village so much in order that there remained nothing but the setting in order of the rest of the world. Her bored eyes wandered sleepily over the assemblage. They seemed to have no preferences for any of them. They rested on the vacuous Bonaparte prince, on the moribund German Jesuit to whom he was listening, on the darkly supple young Spanish priest, on the rosy-gilled English Passionist, on Radet, the writer of that article in the *Revue Rouge*, who was talking to a compatriot in one of the tall windows. She seemed to accept the saturnine-looking men, the political women, who all spoke a language not their own, with an accent and a fluency, and a dangerous far-away smile and a display of questionable teeth all their own. She seemed to class the political with the pious, the obvious adventurer with the seeming fanatic. It was amazing to me to see her there, standing with her county family self-possession in the midst of so much that was questionable. She offered me no explanation; I had to find one for myself.

We stood and talked in the centre of the room. It did not seem a place in which one *could* sit.

"Why have you never been to see me?" she asked languidly. "I might never have known of your existence if it had not been for your sister." My sister was standing at my side, you must remember. I don't suppose that I started, but I made my aunt no answer.

"Indeed," she went on, "I should never have known that you had a sister. Your father was so *very* peculiar. From the day he married, my husband never heard a word from him."

"They were so very different," I said, listlessly.

"Ah, yes," she answered, "brothers so often are." She sighed, apropos of nothing. She continued to utter disjointed sentences from which I gathered a skeleton history of my *soi disant* sister's introduction of herself and of her pretensions. She had, it seemed, casually introduced herself at some garden-party or function of the sort, had represented herself as a sister of my own to whom a maternal uncle had left a fabulous fortune. She herself had suggested her being sheltered under my

"But yesterday . . ." he began in a tone that burlesqued august displeasure. I was wondering what he had looked like on the other side of the door—whilst that lady had been explaining his nature to me.

"Yesterday I wished to avoid embarrassments," I said; "I was to represent your views about Greenland. I might have misunderstood you in some important matter."

"I see, I see," he said conciliatorily. "Yesterday we spoke English for the benefit of the British public. When we speak French we are not in public, I hope." He had a semi-supplicating manner.

"Everything's rather too much in public here," I answered. My part as I imagined it was that of a British brother defending his sister from questionable attentions—the person who "tries to show the man he isn't wanted." But de Mersch didn't see the matter in that light at all. He could not, of course. He was as much used to being purred to as my aunt to looking down on non-county persons. He seemed to think I was making an incomprehensible insular joke, and laughed non-committally. It wouldn't have been possible to let him know he wasn't wanted.

"Oh, you needn't be afraid of my brother," she said suddenly. "He is quite harmless. He is even going to give up writing for the papers except when we want him."

The Duc turned from me to her, smiled and bowed. His smile was inane, but he bowed very well; he had been groomed into that sort of thing or had it in the blood.

"We work together still?" he asked.

"Why not?" she answered.

A hubbub of angry voices raised itself behind my

back. It was one of the *contretemps* that made the Salon Grangeur famous throughout the city.

"You forced yourself upon me. Did I say anywhere
that you were responsible? If it resembles your particular hell upon earth, what is that to me? You do worse
things; you, yourself, monsieur. Haven't I seen . . .
haven't I seen it?"

The Duc de Mersch looked swiftly over his shoulder
toward the window.

"They seem to be angry there," he said nervously.
"Had not something better be done, Miss Granger?"

Miss Granger followed the direction of his eyes.

"Why," she said, "we're used to these differences of
opinion. Besides, it's only Monsieur Radet; he's forever at war with someone or other."

"He ought to be shown the door," the Duc grumbled.

"Oh, as for that," she answered, "we couldn't. My
aunt would be desolated by such a necessity. He is
very influential in certain quarters. My aunt wants to
catch him for the—— He's going to write an article."

"He writes too many articles," the Duc said, with
heavy displeasure.

"Oh, he has written *one* too many," she answered,
"but that can be traversed .· . ."

"But no one believes," the Duc objected . . .
Radet's voice intermittently broke in upon his *sotto voce*,
coming to our ears in gusts.

"Haven't I seen you . . . and then . . .
and you offer me the cross . . . to bribe me to
silence . . . me . . ."

In the general turning of faces toward the window in
which stood Radet and the other, mine turned too.
Radet was a cadaverous, weather-worn, passion-worn
individual, badger-gray, and worked up into a grotesquely attitudinised fury of injured self-esteem. The

other was a denationalised, shifty-eyed, sallow, gray-bearded governor of one of the provinces of the Système Groënlandais; had a closely barbered head, a bull neck, and a great belly. He cast furtive glances round him, uncertain whether to escape or to wait for his say. He looked at the ring that encircled the window at a little distance, and his face, which had betrayed a half-apparent shame, hardened at sight of the cynical masks of the cosmopolitan conspirators. They were amused by the scene. The Holsteiner gained confidence, shrugged his shoulders.

"You have had the fever very badly since you came back," he said, showing a level row of white teeth. "You did not talk like that out there."

"No—*pas si bête*—you would have hanged me, perhaps, as you did that poor devil of a Swiss. What was his name? Now you offer me the cross. Because I had the fever, *hein ?*"

I had been watching the Duc's face; a faint red flush had come creeping from under the roots of his beard, and had spread over the low forehead and the sides of the neck. The eye-glass fell from the eye, a signal for the colour to retreat. The full lips grew pallid, and began to mutter unspoken words. His eyes wandered appealingly from the woman beside him to me. I didn't want to look him in the face. The man was a trafficker in human blood, an evil liver, and I hated him. He had to pay his price; would have to pay—but I didn't want to see him pay it. There was a limit.

I began to excuse myself, and slid out between the groups of excellent plotters. As I was going, she said to me:

"You may come to me to-morrow in the morning."

CHAPTER TWELVE

I was at the Hôtel de Luynes—or Granger—early on the following morning. The mists were still hanging about the dismal upper windows of the inscrutable Faubourg; the toilet of the city was being completed; the little hoses on wheels were clattering about the quiet larger streets. I had not much courage thus early in the day. I had started impulsively; stepping with the impulse of immediate action from the doorstep of the dairy where I had breakfasted. But I made detours; it was too early, and my pace slackened into a saunter as I passed the row of porters' lodges in that dead, inscrutable street. I wanted to fly; had that impulse very strongly; but I burnt my boats with my inquiry of the incredibly ancient, one-eyed porteress. I made my way across the damp courtyard, under the enormous portico, and into the chilly stone hall that no amount of human coming and going sufficed to bring back to a semblance of life. Mademoiselle was expecting me. One went up a great flight of stone steps into one of the immensely high, narrow, impossibly rectangular ante-rooms that one sees in the frontispieces of old plays. The furniture looked no more than knee-high until one discovered that one's self had no appreciable stature. The sad light slanted in ruled lines from the great height of the windows; an army of motes moved slowly in and out of the shadows. I went after awhile and looked disconsolately out into the court-yard. The porteress was making her way across the gravelled space, her arms, her hands, the pockets of her black apron full of letters of all sizes.

I remembered that the *facteur* had followed me down the street. A noise of voices came confusedly to my ears from between half-opened folding-doors; the thing reminded me of my waiting in de Mersch's rooms. It did not last so long. The voices gathered tone, as they do at the end of a colloquy, succeeded each other at longer intervals, and at last came to a sustained halt. The tall doors moved ajar and she entered, followed by a man whom I recognized as the governor of a province of the day before. In that hostile light he looked old and wizened and worried; seemed to have lost much of his rotundity. As for her, she shone with a light of her own.

He greeted me dejectedly, and did not brighten when she let him know that we had a mutual friend in Callan. The Governor, it seemed, in his capacity of Supervisor of the Système, was to conduct that distinguished person through the wilds of Greenland; was to smooth his way and to point out to him excellences of administration.

I wished him a good journey; he sighed and began to fumble with his hat.

"*Alors, c'est entendu,*" she said; giving him leave to depart. He looked at her in an odd sort of way, took her hand and applied it to his lips.

"*C'est entendu,*" he said with a heavy sigh, drops of moisture spattering from beneath his white moustache, "*mais . . .*"

He ogled again with infinitesimal eyes and went out of the room. He had the air of wishing to wipe the perspiration from his brows and to exclaim, "*Quelle femme!*" But if he had any such wish he mastered it until the door hid him from sight.

"Why the . . ." I began before it had well closed, "do you allow that thing to make love to you?" I wanted to take up my position before she could have a chance to make me ridiculous. I wanted to make a long speech—about duty to the name of Granger. But the next word hung, and, before it came, she had answered:

"He?—Oh, I'm making use of him."

"To inherit the earth?" I asked ironically, and she answered gravely:

"To inherit the earth."

She was leaning against the window, playing with the strings of the blinds, and silhouetted against the leaden light. She seemed to be, physically, a little tired; and the lines of her figure to interlace almost tenderly—to "compose" well, after the ideas of a certain school. I knew so little of her—only just enough to be in love with her—that this struck me as the herald of a new phase, not so much in her attitude to me as in mine to her; she had even then a sort of gravity, the gravity of a person on whom things were beginning to weigh.

"But," I said, irresolutely. I could not speak to her; to this new conception of her, in the way I had planned; in the way one would talk to a brilliant, limpid —oh, to a woman of sorts. But I had to take something of my old line. "How would flirting with that man help you?"

"It's quite simple," she answered, "he's to show Callan all Greenland, and Callan is to write . . . Callan has immense influence over a great class, and he will have some of the prestige of—of a Commissioner."

"Oh, I know about Callan," I said.

"And," she went on, "this man had orders to hide things from Callan; you know what it is they have to hide. But he won't now; that is what I was arranging. It's partly by bribery and partly because he has a belief in his *beaux yeux*—so Callan will be upset and will write an . . . exposure; the sort of thing Callan would write if he were well upset. And he will be, by what this man will let him see. You know what a little man like Callan will feel . . . he will be made ill. He would faint at the sight of a drop of blood, you know, and he will see—oh, the very worst, worse than what Radet saw. And he will write a frightful article, and it will be a thunder-clap for de Mersch. . . . And de Mersch will be getting very shaky by then. And your friend Churchill will try to carry de Mersch's railway bill through in the face of the scandal. Churchill's motives will be excellent, but everyone will say . . . You know what people say . . . That is what I and Gurnard want. We want people to talk; we want them to believe . . ."

· I don't know whether there really was a hesitation in her voice, or whether I read that into it. She stood there, playing with the knots of the window cords and speaking in a low monotone. The whole thing, the sad twilight of the place, her tone of voice, seemed tinged with unavailing regret. I had almost forgotten the Dimensionist story, and I had never believed in it. But now, for the first time I began to have my doubts. I was certain that she had been plotting *something* with one of the Duc de Mersch's lieutenants. The man's manner vouched for that; he had not been able to look me in the face. But, more than anything, his voice and manner made me feel that we had passed out of a realm of farcical allegory. I knew enough to see that she might be speaking the truth. And, if she were, her calm avowal of such treachery proved that she *was* what she had said the Dimensionists were; cold, with no scruples, clear-sighted and admirably courageous, and indubitably enemies of society.

"I don't understand," I said. "But de Mersch then?"

She made a little gesture; one of those movements that I best remember of her; the smallest, the least noticeable. It reduced de Mersch to nothing; he no longer even counted.

"Oh, as for him," she said, "he is only a detail." I had still the idea that she spoke with a pitying intonation—as if she were speaking to a dog in pain. "He doesn't really count; not really. He will crumble up and disappear, very soon. You won't even remember him."

"But," I said, "you go about with him, as if you . . . You are getting yourself talked about . . . Everyone thinks—" . . . The accusation that I had come to make seemed impossible, now I was facing her. "I believe," I added, with the suddenness of inspiration. "I'm certain even, that *he* thinks that you . . ."

"Well, they think that sort of thing. But it is only part of the game. Oh, I assure you it is no more than that."

I was silent. I felt that, for one reason or another, she wished me to believe.

"Yes," she said, "I want you to believe. It will save you a good deal of pain."

"If you wanted to save me pain," I maintained, "you would have done with de Mersch . . . for good." I had an idea that the solution was beyond me. It was as if the controlling powers were flitting, invisible, just above my head, just beyond my grasp. There was obviously something vibrating; some cord, somewhere, stretched very taut and quivering. But I could think of no better solution than: "You must have done with him." It seemed obvious, too, that that was impossi-

ble, was outside the range of things that could be done
—but I had to do my best. "It's a—it's vile," I added,
"vile."

"Oh, I know, I know," she said, "for you . . .
And I'm even sorry. But it has to be gone on with.
De Mersch has to go under in just this way. It can't
be any other."

"Why not?" I asked, because she had paused. I
hadn't any desire for enlightenment.

"It isn't even only Churchill," she said, "not even
only that de Mersch will bring down Churchill with him.
It is that he must bring down everything that Churchill
stands for. You know what that is—the sort of probity, all the old order of things. And the more vile the
means used to destroy de Mersch the more vile the whole
affair will seem. People—the sort of people—have an
idea that a decent man cannot be touched by tortuous
intrigues. And the whole thing will be—oh, malodor-
ous. You understand."

"I don't," I answered, "I don't understand at
all."

"Ah, yes, you do," she said, "you understand . . ."
She paused for a long while, and I was silent. I understood vaguely what she meant; that if Churchill fell
amid the clouds of dust of such a collapse, there would
be an end of belief in probity . . . or nearly an
end. But I could not see what it all led up to; where it
left us.

"You see," she began again, "I want to make it as
little painful to you as I can; as little painful as explanations *can* make it. I can't feel as you feel, but I can see,
rather dimly, what it is that hurts you. And so . . .
I want to; I really want to."

"But you won't do the one thing," I returned hopelessly to the charge.

"I cannot," she answered, "it must be like that; there isn't any way. You are so tied down to these little things. Don't you see that de Mersch, and—and all these people—don't really count? They aren't anything at all in the scheme of things. I think that, even for you, they aren't worth bothering about. They're only accidents; the accidents that——"

"That what?" I asked, although I began to see dimly what she meant.

"That lead in the inevitable," she answered. "Don't you see? Don't you understand? We *are* the inevitable . . . and you can't keep us back. We have to come and you, you will only hurt yourself, by resisting." A sense that this was the truth, the only truth, beset me. It was for the moment impossible to think of anything else—of anything else in the world. "You must accept us and all that we mean, you must stand back; sooner or later. Look even all round you, and you will understand better. You are in the house of a type—a type that became impossible. Oh, centuries ago. And that type too, tried very hard to keep back the inevitable; not only because itself went under, but because everything that it stood for went under. And it had to suffer—heartache . . . that sort of suffering. Isn't it so?"

I did not answer; the illustration was too abominably just. It was just that. There were even now all these people—these Legitimists—sneering ineffectually; shutting themselves away from the light in their mournful houses and suffering horribly because everything that they stood for had gone under.

"But even if I believe you," I said, "the thing is too horrible, and your tools are too mean; that man who has just gone out and—and Callan—are they the weapons of the inevitable? After all, the Revolution . . ."

I was striving to get back to tangible ideas—ideas that one could name and date and label . . . "the Revolution was noble in essence and made for good. But all this of yours is too vile and too petty. You are bribing, or something worse, that man to betray his master. And that you call helping on the inevitable . . ."

"They used to say just that of the Revolution. That wasn't nice of its tools. Don't you see? They were the people that went under . . . They couldn't see the good . . ."

"And I—I am to take it on trust," I said, bitterly.

"You couldn't see the good," she answered, "it isn't possible, and there is no way of explaining. Our languages are different, and there's no bridge—no bridge at all. We *can't* meet . . ."

It was that revolted me. If there was no bridge and we could not meet, we must even fight; that is, if I believed her version of herself. If I did not, I was being played the fool with. I preferred to think that. If she were only fooling me she remained attainable. If it was as she said, there was no hope at all—not any.

"I don't believe you," I said, suddenly. I didn't want to believe her. The thing was too abominable— too abominable for words, and incredible. I struggled against it as one struggles against inevitable madness, against the thought of it. It hung over me, stupefying, deadening. One could only fight it with violence, crudely, in jerks, as one struggles against the numbness of frost. It was like a pall, like descending clouds of smoke, seemed to be actually present in the absurdly lofty room—this belief in what she stood for, in what she said she stood for.

"I don't believe you," I proclaimed, "I won't . . .

You are playing the fool with me . . . trying to get round me . . . to make me let you go on with these—with these—— It is abominable. Think of what it means for me, what people are saying of me, and I am a decent man—— You shall not. Do you understand, you *shall* not. It is unbearable . . . and you . . . you try to fool me . . . in order to keep me quiet . . ."

"Oh, no," she said. "Oh, no."

She had an accent that touched grief, as nearly as she could touch it. I remember it now, as one remembers these things. But then I passed it over. I was too much moved myself to notice it more than subconsciously, as one notices things past which one is whirled. And I was whirled past these things, in an ungovernable fury at the remembrance of what I had suffered, of what I had still to suffer. I was speaking with intense rage, jerking out words, ideas, as floodwater jerks through a sluice the *débris* of once ordered fields.

"You are," I said, "you *are*—you—you—dragging an ancient name through the dust—you . . ."

I forget what I said. But I remember, "dragging an ancient name." It struck me, at the time, by its for-lornness, as part of an appeal to her. It was so patheti-cally tiny a motive, so out of tone, that it stuck in my mind. I only remember the upshot of my speech; that, unless she swore—oh, yes, swore—to have done with de Mersch, I would denounce her to my aunt at that very moment and in that very house.

And she said that it was impossible.

CHAPTER THIRTEEN

I HAD a sense of walking very fast—almost of taking flight—down a long dim corridor, and of a door that opened into an immense room. All that I remember of it, as I saw it then, was a number of pastel portraits of weak, vacuous individuals, in dulled, gilt, oval frames. The heads stood out from the panelling and stared at me from between ringlets, from under powdered hair, simpering, or contemptuous with the expression that must have prevailed in the *monde* of the time before the Revolution. At a great distance, bent over account-books and pink cheques on the flap of an escritoire, sat my aunt, very small, very gray, very intent on her work.

The people who built these rooms must have had some property of the presence to make them bulk large —if they ever really did so—in the eyes of dependents, of lackeys. Perhaps it was their sense of ownership that gave them the necessary prestige. My aunt, who was only a temporary occupant, certainly had none of it. Bent intently over her accounts, peering through her spectacles at columns of figures, she was nothing but a little old woman alone in an immense room. It seemed impossible that she could really have any family pride, any pride of any sort. She looked round at me over her spectacles, across her shoulder.

"Ah . . . Etchingham," she said. She seemed to be trying to carry herself back to England, to the England of her land-agent and her select visiting list. Here she was no more superior than if we had been on a desert island. I wanted to enlighten her as to the woman she was sheltering—wanted to very badly; but a necessity for introducing the matter seemed to arise as she gradually stiffened into assertiveness.

"My dear aunt," I said, "the woman . . ." The alien nature of the theme grew suddenly formidable. She looked at me arousedly.

"You got my note then," she said. "But I don't think a woman *can* have brought it. I have given such strict orders. They have such strange ideas here, though. And Madame—the *portière*—is an old retainer of M. de Luynes, I haven't much influence over her. It is absurd, but . . ." It seems that the old lady in the lodge made a point of carrying letters that went by hand. She had an eye for gratuities—and the police, I should say, were concerned. They make a good deal of use of that sort of person in that neighbourhood of infinitesimal and unceasing plotting.

"I didn't mean that," I said, "but the woman who calls herself my sister . . ."

"My dear nephew," she interrupted, with tranquil force, as if she were taking an arranged line, "I cannot—I absolutely cannot be worried with your quarrels with your sister. As I said to you in my note of this morning, when you are in this town you must consider this house your home. It is almost insulting of you to go to an inn. I am told it is even . . . quite an unfit place that you are stopping at—for a member of our family."

I maintained for a few seconds a silence of astonishment.

"But," I returned to the charge, "the matter is one of importance. You must understand that she . . ."

My aunt stiffened and froze. It was as if I had committed some flagrant sin against etiquette.

"If I am satisfied as to her behaviour," she said, "I think that you might be." She paused as if she were satisfied that she had set me hopelessly in the wrong.

"I don't withdraw my invitation," she said. "You must understand I *wish* you to come here. But your quarrels you and she must settle. On those terms. . . ."

She had the air of conferring an immense favour, as if she believed that I had, all my life through, been waiting for her invitation to come within the pale. As for me, I felt a certain relief at having the carrying out of my duty made impossible for me. I did not *want* to tell my aunt and thus to break things off definitely and for good. Something would have happened; the air might have cleared as it clears after a storm; I should have learnt where I stood. But I was afraid of the knowledge. Light in these dark places might reveal an abyss at my feet. I wanted to let things slide.

My aunt had returned to her accounts, the accounts which were the cog-wheels that kept running the smooth course of the Etchingham estates. She seemed to wish to indicate that I counted for not very much in the scheme of things as she saw it.

"I should like to make your better acquaintance," she said, with her head still averted, "there are reasons . . ." It came suddenly into my head that she had an idea of testamentary dispositions, that she felt she was breaking up, that I had my rights. I didn't much care for the thing, but the idea of being the heir of Etchingham was—well, was an idea. It would make me more possible to my pseudo-sister. It would be, as it were, a starting-point, would make me potentially a somebody of her sort of ideal. Moreover, I should be under the same roof, near her, with her sometimes. One asks so little more than that, that it seemed almost

half the battle. I began to consider phrases of thanks
and acceptance and then uttered them.

I never quite understood the bearings of that scene;
never quite whether my aunt really knew that my sister
was not my sister. She was a wonderfully clever woman
of the unscrupulous order, with a *sang-froid* and self-
possession well calculated to let her cut short any in-
convenient revelations. It was as if she had had long
practice in the art, though I cannot say what occasion she can have had for its practice—perhaps for
the confounding of wavering avowers of Dissent at
home.

I used to think that she knew, if not all, at least a
portion; that the weight that undoubtedly was upon her
mind was nothing else but that. She broke up, was
breaking up from day to day, and I can think of no
other reason. She had the air of being disintegrated,
like a mineral under an immense weight—quartz in a
crushing mill; of being dulled and numbed as if she were
under the influence of narcotics.

There is little enough wonder, if she actually carried
that imponderable secret about with her. I used to
look at her sometimes, and wonder if she, too, saw the
oncoming of the inevitable. She was limited enough in
her ideas, but not too stupid to take that in if it pre-
sented itself. Indeed they have that sort of idea rather
grimly before them all the time—that class.

It must have been that that was daily, and little
by little, pressing down her eyelids and deepening the
quivering lines of her impenetrable face. She had a
certain solitary grandeur, the pathos attaching to the
last of a race, of a type; the air of waiting for the deluge,
of listening for an inevitable sound—the sound of oncoming waters.

It was weird, the time that I spent in that house—

more than weird—deadening.   It had an extraordinary
effect on me—an effect that my "sister", perhaps, had
carefully calculated.   She made pretensions of that sort
later on; said that she had been breaking me in to per-
form my allotted task in the bringing on of the inevitable.

I have nowhere come across such an intense solitude
as there was there, a solitude that threw one so absolutely upon one's self and into one's self.   I used to sit
working in one of those tall, panelled rooms, very high
up in the air.   I was writing at the series of articles for
the *Bi-Monthly*, for Polehampton.   I was to get the
atmosphere of Paris, you remember.   It was rather
extraordinary, that process.   Up there I seemed to be
as much isolated from Paris as if I had been in—well,
in Hampton Court.   It was almost impossible to write;
I had things to think about: preoccupations, jealousies.
It was true I had a living to make, but that seemed to
have lost its engrossingness as a pursuit, or at least to
have suspended it.

The panels of the room seemed to act as a sounding-
board, the belly of an immense 'cello.   There were
never any noises in the house, only whispers coming
from an immense distance—as when one drops stones
down an unfathomable well and hears ages afterward
the faint sound of disturbed waters.   When I look back
at that time I figure myself as forever sitting with up-
lifted pen, waiting for a word that would not come, and
that I did not much care about getting.   The panels of
the room would creak sympathetically to the opening of
the entrance-door of the house, the faintest of creaks;
people would cross the immense hall to the room in
which they plotted; would cross leisurely, with laughter
and rustling of garments that after a long time reached
my ears in whispers.   Then I would have an access of

mad jealousy. I wanted to be part of her life, but I could not stand that Salon of suspicious conspirators. What could I do there? Stand and look at them, conscious that they all dropped their voices instinctively when I came near them?

That was the general tone of that space of time, but, of course, it was not always that. I used to emerge now and then to breakfast sympathetically with my aunt, sometimes to sit through a meal with the two of them. I danced attendance on them singly; paid depressing calls with my aunt; calls on the people in the Faubourg; people without any individuality other than a kind of desiccation, the shrivelled appearance and point of view of a dried pippin. In revenge, they had names that startled one, names that recalled the generals and *flaneurs* of an impossibly distant time; names that could hardly have had any existence outside the memoirs of Madame de Sévigné, the names of people that could hardly have been fitted to do anything more vigorous than be reflected in the mirrors of the *Salle des Glaces*. I was so absolutely depressed, so absolutely in a state of suspended animation, that I seemed to conform exactly to my aunt's ideas of what was desirable in me as an attendant on her at these functions. I used to stand behind chairs and talk, like a good young man, to the assorted *Pères* and *Abbés* who were generally present.

And then I used to go home and get the atmospheres of these people. I must have done it abominably badly, for the notes that brought Polchampton's cheques were accompanied by the bravos of that gentleman and the assurances that Miss Polehampton liked my work—liked it very much.

I suppose I exhibited myself in the capacity of the man who knew—who could let you into a thing or two.

After all, any one could write about students' balls and the lakes in the Bois, but it took *someone* to write "with knowledge" of the interiors of the barred houses in the Rue de l' Université.

Then, too, I attended the more showy entertainments with my sister. I had by now become so used to hearing her styled "your sister" that the epithet had the quality of a name. She was "mademoiselle votre sœur," as she might have been Mlle. Patience or Hope, without having anything of the named quality. What she did at the entertainments, the charitable bazaars, the dismal dances, the impossibly bad concerts, I had no idea. She must have had some purpose, for she did nothing without. I myself descended into fulfilling the functions of a rudimentarily developed chaperon— functions similar in importance to those performed by the eyes of a mole. I had the maddest of accesses of jealousy if she talked to a man—and *such* men—or danced with one. And then I was forever screwing my courage up and feeling it die away. We used to drive about in a coupé, a thing that shut us inexorably together, but which quite as inexorably destroyed all opportunities for what one calls making love. In smooth streets its motion was too glib, on the *pavé* it rattled too abominably. I wanted to make love to her —oh, immensely, but I was never in the mood, or the opportunity was never forthcoming. I used to have the wildest fits of irritation; not of madness or of depression, but of simple wildness at the continual recurrence of small obstacles. I couldn't read, couldn't bring myself to it. I used to sit and look dazedly at the English newspapers—at any newspaper but the *Hour*. De Mersch had, for the moment, disappeared. There were troubles in his elective grand duchy—he had, indeed, contrived to make himself unpopular with the electors, excessively unpopular. I used to read piquant articles about his embroglio in an American paper that devoted itself to matters of the sort. All sorts of international difficulties were to arise if de Mersch were ejected. There was some other obscure prince of a rival house, Prussian or Russian, who had desires for the degree of royalty that sat so heavily on de Mersch. Indeed, I think there were two rival princes, each waiting with portmanteaux packed and manifestos in their breast pockets, ready to pass de Mersch's frontiers.

The grievances of his subjects—so the Paris-American *Gazette* said—were intimately connected with matters of finance, and de Mersch's personal finances and his grand ducal were inextricably mixed up with the wildcat schemes with which he was seeking to make a fortune large enough to enable him to laugh at half a dozen elective grand duchies. Indeed, de Mersch's own portmanteau was reported to be packed against the day when British support of his Greenland schemes would let him afford to laugh at his cantankerous Diet.

The thing interested me so little that I never quite mastered the details of it. I wished the man no good, but so long as he kept out of my way I was not going to hate him actively. Finally the affairs of Holstein-Launewitz ceased to occupy the papers—the thing was arranged and the Russian and Prussian princes unpacked their portmanteaux, and, I suppose, consigned their manifestos to the flames, or adapted them to the needs of other principalities. De Mersch's affairs ceded their space in the public prints to the topic of the dearness of money. Somebody, somewhere, was said to be up to something. I used to try to read the articles, to master the details, because I disliked finding a whole field of thought of which I knew absolutely nothing. I used to read about the great discount houses and other things that conveyed absolutely nothing to my mind. I only gathered that the said great houses were having a very bad time, and that everybody else was having a very much worse.

One day, indeed, the matter was brought home to me by the receipt from Polehampton of bills instead of my usual cheques. I had a good deal of trouble in cashing the things; indeed, people seemed to look askance at them. I consulted my aunt on the subject, at breakfast. It was the sort of thing that interested the woman of business in her, and we were always short of topics of conversation.

We breakfasted in rather a small room, as rooms went there; my aunt sitting at the head of the table, with an early morning air of being *en famille* that she wore at no other time of day. It was not a matter of garments, for she was not the woman to wear a *peignoir;* but lay, I supposed, in her manner, which did not begin to assume frigidity until several watches of the day had passed.

I handed her Polehampton's bills and explained that I was at a loss to turn them to account; that I even had only the very haziest of ideas as to their meaning. Holding the forlorn papers in her hand, she began to lecture me on the duty of acquiring the rudiments of what she called "business habits."

"Of course you do not require to master details to any considerable extent," she said, "but I always have held that it is one of the duties of a . . ."

She interrupted herself as my sister came into the room; looked at her, and then held out the papers in her hand. The things quivered a little; the hand must have quivered too.

"You are going to Halderschrodt's?" she said, interrogatively. "You could get him to negotiate these for Etchingham?"

Miss Granger looked at the papers negligently.

"I am going this afternoon," she answered. "Etchingham can come . . ." She suddenly turned to me: "So your friend is getting shaky," she said.

"It means that?" I asked. "But I've heard that he has done the same sort of thing before."

"He must have been shaky before," she said, "but I daresay Halderschrodt . . ."

"Oh, it's hardly worth while bothering that personage about such a sum," I interrupted. Halderschrodt, in those days, was a name that suggested no dealings in any sum less than a million.

"My dear Etchingham," my aunt interrupted in a shocked tone, "it is quite worth his while to oblige us . . ."

"I didn't know," I said.

That afternoon we drove to Halderschrodt's private office, a sumptuous—that is the *mot juste*—suite of rooms on the first floor of the house next to the Duc de Mersch's *Sans Souci*. I sat on a plush-bottomed gilded chair, whilst my pseudo-sister transacted her business in an adjoining room—a room exactly corresponding with that within which de Mersch had lurked whilst the lady was warning me against him. A clerk came after a while, carried me off into an enclosure, where my bill was discounted by another, and then reconducted me to my plush chair. I did not occupy it, as it happened. A meagre, very tall Alsatian was holding the door open for the exit of my sister. He said nothing at all, but stood slightly inclined as she passed him. I caught a glimpse of a red, long face, very tired eyes, and hair of almost startling whiteness—the white hair of a comparatively young man, without any lustre of any sort—a dead white, like that of snow. I remember that white hair with a feeling of horror, whilst I have almost forgotten the features of the great Baron de Halder-schrodt.

I had still some of the feeling of having been in contact with a personality of the most colossal significance as we went down the red carpet of the broad white marble stairs. With one foot on the lowest step, the figure of a perfectly clothed, perfectly groomed man was standing looking upward at our descent. I had thought so little of him that the sight of the Duc de Mersch's face hardly suggested any train of emotions. It lit up with an expression of pleasure.

"You," he said.

She stood looking down upon him from the altitude of two steps, looking with intolerable passivity.

"So you use the common stairs," she said; "one had the idea that you communicated with these people through a private door." He laughed uneasily, looking askance at me.

"Oh, I . . ." he said.

She moved a little to one side to pass him in her descent.

"So things have arranged themselves—*là bas*," she said, referring, I supposed, to the elective grand duchy.

"Oh, it was like a miracle," he answered, "and I owed a great deal—a great deal—to your hints . . ."

"You must tell me all about it to-night," she said.

De Mersch's face had an extraordinary quality that I seemed to notice in all the faces around me—a quality of the flesh that seemed to lose all luminosity, of the eyes that seemed forever to have a tendency to seek the ground, to avoid the sight of the world. When he brightened to answer her it was as if with effort. It seemed as if a weight were on the mind of the whole world—a preoccupation that I shared without understanding. She herself, a certain absent-mindedness apart, seemed the only one that was entirely unaffected.

As we sat side by side in the little carriage, she said suddenly:

"They are coming to the end of their tether, you see." I shrank away from her a little—but I did not see and did not want to see. I said so. It even seemed to me that de Mersch having got over the troubles *là bas*, was taking a new lease of life.

"I *did* think," I said, "a little time ago that　.　.　."

The wheels of the coupé suddenly began to rattle abominably over the cobbles of a narrow street. It was impossible to talk, and I was thrown back upon myself. I found that I was in a temper—in an abominable temper. The sudden sight of that man, her method of greeting him, the intimacy that the scene revealed . . . the whole thing had upset me. Of late, for want of any alarms, in spite of groundlessness I had had the impression that I was the integral part of her life. It was not a logical idea, but strictly a habit of mind that had grown up in the desolation of my solitude.

We passed into one of the larger boulevards, and the thing ran silently.

"That de Mersch was crumbling up," she suddenly completed my unfinished sentence; "oh, that was only a grumble—premonitory. But it won't take long now. I have been putting on the screw. Halderschrodt will . . . I suppose he will commit suicide, in a day or two. And then the—the fun will begin."

I didn't answer. The thing made no impression—no mental impression at all.

CHAPTER FOURTEEN

THAT afternoon we had a scene, and late that night another. The memory of the former is a little blotted out. Things began to move so quickly that, try as I will to arrange their sequence in my mind, I cannot. I cannot even very distinctly remember what she told me at that first explanation. I must have attacked her fiercely—on the score of de Mersch, in the old vein; must have told her that I would not in the interest of the name allow her to see the man again. She told me things, too, rather abominable things, about the way in which she had got Halderschrodt into her power and was pressing him down. Halderschrodt was de Mersch's banker-in-chief; his fall would mean de Mersch's, and so on. The "so on" in this case meant a great deal more. Halderschrodt, apparently was the "somebody who was up to something" of the American paper—that is to say the allied firms that Halderschrodt represented. I can't remember the details. They were too huge and too unfamiliar, and I was too agitated by my own share in the humanity of it. But, in sum, it seemed that the fall of Halderschrodt would mean a sort of incredibly vast Black Monday—a frightful thing in the existing state of public confidence, but one which did not mean much to me. I forget how she said she had been able to put the screw on him. Halderschrodt, as you must remember, was the third of his colossal name, a man without much genius and conscious of the lack, obsessed with the idea of operating some enormous coup, like the founder of his dynasty, something in which foresight in international occurrence played a chief part. That idea was his weakness, the defect of his mind, and she had played on that weakness. I forget, I say, the details, if I ever heard them; they concerned themselves with a dynastic revolution somewhere, a revolution that was to cause a slump all over the world, and that had been engineered in our Salon. And she had burked the revolution—betrayed it, I suppose—and the consequences did not ensue, and Halderschrodt and all the rest of them were left high and dry.

The whole thing was a matter of under-currents that never came to the surface, a matter of shifting sands from which only those with the clearest heads could come forth.

"And we . . . we have clear heads," she said. It was impossible to listen to her without shuddering. For me, if he stood for anything, Halderschrodt stood for stability; there was the tremendous name, and there was the person I had just seen, the person on whom a habit of mind approaching almost to the royal had conferred a presence that had some of the divinity that hedges a king. It seemed frightful merely to imagine his ignominious collapse; as frightful as if she had pointed out a splendid-limbed man and said: "That man will be dead in five minutes." That, indeed, was what she said of Halderschrodt . . . The man had saluted her, going to his death; the austere inclination that I had seen had been the salutation of such a man.

I was so moved by one thing and another that I hardly noticed that Gurnard had come into the room. I had not seen him since the night when he had dined with the Duc de Mersch at Churchill's, but he seemed so part of the emotion, of the frame of mind, that he slid noiselessly into the scene and hardly surprised me. I was called out of the room—someone desired to see me, and I passed, without any transition of feeling, into the presence of an entire stranger—a man who remains a voice to me. He began to talk to me about the state of my aunt's health. He said she was breaking up; that he begged respectfully to urge that I would use my influence to take her back to London to consult Sir James —I, perhaps, living in the house and not having known my aunt for very long, might not see; but he . . . He was my aunt's solicitor. He was quite right; my aunt *was* breaking up, she had declined visibly in the few hours that I had been away from her. She had been doing business with this man, had altered her will, had seen Mr. Gurnard; and, in some way had received a shock that seemed to have deprived her of all volition. She sat with her head leaning back, her eyes closed, the lines of her face all seeming to run downward.

"It is obvious to me that arrangements ought to be made for your return to England," the lawyer said, "whatever engagements Miss Granger or Mr. Etchingham Granger or even Mr. Gurnard may have made."

I wondered vaguely what the devil Mr. Gurnard could have to say in the matter, and then Miss Granger herself came into the room.

"They want me," my aunt said in a low voice, "they have been persuading me . . . to go back . . . to Etchingham, I think you said, Meredith."

I became conscious that I wanted to return to England, wanted it very much, wanted to be out of this; to get somewhere where there was stability and things that one could understand. Everything here seemed to be in a mist, with the ground trembling underfoot.

"Why . . ." Miss Granger's verdict came, "we can go when you like. To-morrow."

Things immediately began to shape themselves on

these unexpected lines, a sort of bustle of departure to be in the air. I was employed to conduct the lawyer as far as the porter's lodge, a longish traverse. He beguiled the way by excusing himself for hurrying back to London.

"I might have been of use; in these hurried departures there are generally things. But, you will understand, Mr.—Mr. Etchingham; at a time like this I could hardly spare the hours that it cost me to come over. You would be astonished what a deal of extra work it gives and how far-spreading the evil is. People seem to have gone mad. Even I have been astonished."

"I had no idea," I said.

"Of course not, of course not—no one had. But, unless I am much mistaken—*much*—there will have to be an enquiry, and people will be very lucky who have had nothing to do with it . . ."

I gathered that things were in a bad way, over there, as over here; that there were scandals and a tremendous outcry for purification in the highest places. I saw the man get into his fiacre and took my way back across the court-yard rather slowly, pondering over the part I was to fill in the emigration, wondering how far events had conferred on me a partnership in the family affairs.

I found that my tacitly acknowledged function was that of supervising nurse-tender, the sort of thing that made for personal tenderness in the aridity of profuse hired help. I was expected to arrange a rug just a *little* more comfortably than the lady's maid who would travel in the compartment—to give the finishing touches.

It was astonishing how well the thing was engineered; the removal, I mean. It gave me an even better idea of the woman my aunt had been than had the panic of her solicitor. The thing went as smoothly as the disappearance of a caravan of gypsies, camped for the night on a heath beside gorse bushes. We went to the ball that night as if from a household that had its roots deep in the solid rock, and in the morning we had disappeared.

The ball itself was a finishing touch—the finishing touch of my sister's affairs and the end of my patience. I spent an interminable night, one of those nights that never end and that remain quivering and raw in the memory. I seemed to be in a blaze of light, watching, through a shifting screen of shimmering dresses—her and the Duc de Mersch. I don't know whether the thing was really noticeable, but it seemed that everyone was—that everyone must be—remarking it. I thought I caught women making smile-punctuated remarks behind fans, men answering inaudibly with eyes discreetly on the ground. It was a mixed assembly, somebody's liquidation of social obligations, and there was a sprinkling of the kind of people who do make remarks. It was not the noticeability for its own sake that I hated, but the fact that their relations by their noticeability made me impossible, whilst the notice itself confirmed my own fears. I hung, glowering in corners, noticeable enough myself, I suppose.

The thing reached a crisis late in the evening. There was a kind of winter-garden that one strolled in, a place of giant palms stretching up into a darkness of intense shadow. I was prowling about in the shadows of great metallic leaves, cursing under my breath, in a fury of nervous irritation; quivering like a horse martyrised by a stupidly, merciless driver. I happened to stand back for a moment in the narrowest of paths, with the touch of spiky leaves on my hand and on my face. In front of me was the glaring perspective of one of the longer alleys, and, stepping into it, a great band of blue ribbon cutting across his chest, came de Mersch with her upon his arm. De Mersch himself hardly counted. He had a way of glowing, but he paled ineffectual fires besides her mænadic glow. There was something over-powering in the sight of her, in the fire of her eyes, in the glow of her coils of hair, in the poise of her head. She wore some kind of early nineteenth-century dress, sweeping low from the waist with a tenderness of fold that affected one with delicate pathos, that had a virgin quality of almost poignant intensity. And beneath it she stepped with the buoyancy—the long steps—of a triumphing Diana.

It was more than terrible for me to stand there longing with a black, baffled longing, with some of the base quality of an eavesdropper and all the baseness of the unsuccessful.

Then Gurnard loomed in the distance, moving insensibly down the long, glaring corridor, a sinister figure, suggesting in the silence of his oncoming the motionless flight of a vulture. Well within my field of sight he overtook them and, with a lack of preliminary greeting that suggested supreme intimacy, walked beside them. I stood for some moments—for some minutes, and then hastened after them. I was going to do something. After a time I found de Mersch and Gurnard standing facing each other in one of the doorways of the place— Gurnard, a small, dark, impassive column; de Mersch, bulky, overwhelming, florid, standing with his legs well apart and speaking vociferously with a good deal of gesture. I approached them from the side, standing rather insistently at his elbow.

"I want," I said, "I would be extremely glad if you would give me a minute, monsieur." I was conscious that I spoke with a tremor of the voice, a sort of throaty eagerness. I was unaware of what course I was

to pursue, but I was confident of calmness, of self-control
—I was equal to that.   They had a pause of surprised
silence.   Gurnard wheeled and fixed me critically with
his eye-glass.   I took de Mersch a little apart, into a
solitude of palm branches, and began to speak before
he had asked me my errand.

"You must understand that I would not interfere
without a good deal of provocation," I was saying, when
he cut me short, speaking in a thick, jovial voice.

"Oh, we will understand that, my good Granger, and
then . . ."

"It is about my sister," I said—"you—you go too far.
I must ask you, as a gentleman, to cease persecuting
her."

He answered "The devil!" and then: "If I do
not——?"

It was evident in his voice, in his manner, that the
man was a little—well, *gris*.   "If you do not," I said,
"I shall forbid her to see you and I shall . . ."

"Oh, oh!" he interjected with the intonation of a
reveller at a farce.   "We are at that—we are the excellent brother."   He paused, and then added: "Well,
go to the devil, you and your forbidding."   He spoke
with the greatest good humour.

"I am in earnest," I said; "very much in earnest.
The thing has gone too far, and even for your own sake,
you had better . . ."

He said "Ah, ah!" in the tone of his "Oh, oh!"

"She is no friend to you," I struggled on, "she is
playing with you for her own purposes; you will . . ."

He swayed a little on his feet and said: "Bravo
. . . bravissimo.   If we can't forbid him, we will
frighten him.   Go on, my good fellow . . ." and
then, "Come, go on . . ."

I looked at his great bulk of a body.   It came into

my head dimly that I wanted him to strike me, to give me an excuse—anything to end the scene violently, with a crash and exclamations of fury.

"You absolutely refuse to pay any attention?" I said.

"Oh, absolutely," he answered.

"You know that I can do something, that I can expose you." I had a vague idea that I could, that the number of small things that I knew to his discredit and the mass of my hatred could be welded into a damning whole. He laughed a high-pitched, hysterical laugh. The dawn was beginning to spread pallidly above us, gleaming mournfully through the glass of the palm-house. People began to pass, muffled up, on their way out of the place.

"You may go . . ." he was beginning. But the expression of his face altered. Miss Granger, muffled up like all the rest of the world, was coming out of the inner door. "We have been having a charming . . ." he began to her. She touched me gently on the arm.

"Come, Arthur," she said, and then to him, "You have heard the news?"

He looked at her rather muzzily.

"Baron Halderschrodt has committed suicide," she said. "Come, Arthur."

We passed on slowly, but de Mersch followed.

"You—you aren't in *earnest?*" he said, catching at her arm so that we swung round and faced him. There was a sort of mad entreaty in his eyes, as if he hoped that by unsaying she could remedy an irremediable disaster, and there was nothing left of him but those panic-stricken, beseeching eyes.

"Monsieur de Sabran told me," she answered; "he had just come from making the *constatation*. Besides, you can hear . . ."

Half-sentences came to our ears from groups that

passed us. A very old man with a nose that almost touched his thick lips, was saying to another of the same type:

"Shot himself . . . through the left temple . . . *Mon Dieu!*"

De Mersch walked slowly down the long corridor away from us. There was an extraordinary stiffness in his gait, as if he were trying to emulate the goose step of his days in the Prussian Guard. My companion looked after him as though she wished to gauge the extent of his despair.

"You would say '*Habet*', wouldn't you?" she asked me.

I thought we had seen the last of him, but as in the twilight of the dawn we waited for the lodge gates to open, a furious clatter of hoofs came down the long street, and a carriage drew level with ours. A moment after, de Mersch was knocking at our window.

"You will . . . you will . . ." he stuttered, "speak . . . to Mr. Gurnard. That is our only chance . . . now." His voice came in mingled with the cold air of the morning. I shivered. "You have so much power . . . with him and . . ."

"Oh, I . . ." she answered.

"The thing must go through," he said again, "or else . . ." He paused. The great gates in front of us swung noiselessly open, one saw into the court-yard. The light was growing stronger. She did not answer.

"I tell you," he asseverated insistently, "if the British Government abandons my railway *all* our plans . . ."

"Oh, the Government won't *abandon* it," she said, with a little emphasis on the verb. He stepped back out of range of the wheels, and we turned in and left him standing there.

.   .   .   .

In the great room which was usually given up to the political plotters stood a table covered with eatables and lit by a pair of candles in tall silver sticks. I was conscious of a raging hunger and of a fierce excitement that made the thought of sleep part of a past of phantoms. I began to eat unconsciously, pacing up and down the while. She was standing beside the table in the glow of the transparent light. Pallid blue lines showed in the long windows. It was very cold and hideously late; away in those endless small hours when the pulse drags, when the clock-beat drags, when time is effaced.

"You see?" she said suddenly.

"Oh, I see," I answered—"and . . . and now?"

"Now we are almost done with each other," she answered.

I felt a sudden mental falling away. I had never looked at things in that way, had never really looked things in the face. I had grown so used to the idea that she was to parcel out the remainder of my life, had grown so used to the feeling that I was the integral portion of her life . . . "But I——" I said. "What is to become of me?"

She stood looking down at the ground . . . for a long time. At last she said in a low monotone:

"Oh, you must try to forget."

A new idea struck me—luminously, overwhelming. I grew reckless. "You—you are growing considerate," I taunted. "You are not so sure, not so cold. I notice a change in you. Upon my soul . . ."

Her eyes dilated suddenly, and as suddenly closed again. She said nothing. I grew conscious of unbearable pain, the pain of returning life. She was going away. I should be alone. The future began to exist again, looming up like a vessel through thick mist, silent, phantasmal, overwhelming—a hideous future of irremediable remorse, of solitude, of craving.

"You are going back to work with Churchill," she said suddenly.

"How did you know?" I asked breathlessly. My despair of a sort found vent in violent interjecting of an immaterial query.

"You leave your letters about," she said, "and . . . It will be best for you."

"It will not," I said bitterly. "It could never be the same. I don't want to see Churchill. I want . . ."

"You want?" she asked, in a low monotone.

"You," I answered.

She spoke at last, very slowly:

"Oh, as for me, I am going to marry Gurnard."

I don't know just what I said then, but I remember that I found myself repeating over and over again, the phrases running metrically up and down my mind: "You couldn't marry Gurnard; you don't know what he is. You couldn't marry Gurnard; you don't know what he is." I don't suppose that I knew anything to the discredit of Gurnard—but he struck me in that way at that moment; struck me convincingly—more than any array of facts could have done.

"Oh—as for what he is——" she said, and paused. "*I* know . . ." and then suddenly she began to speak very fast.

"Don't you see?—*can't* you see?—that I don't marry Gurnard for what he is in that sense, but for what he is in the other. It isn't a marriage in your sense at all. And . . . and it doesn't affect you . . . don't you *see?* We have to have done with one another, because . . . because . . ."

I had an inspiration.

"I believe," I said, very slowly, "I believe . . . you *do* care. . . ."

She said nothing.

"You care," I repeated.

She spoke then with an energy that had something of a threat in it. "Do you think I would? Do you think I could? . . . or dare? Don't you understand?" She faltered—"but then . . ." she added, and was silent for a long minute. I felt the throb of a thousand pulses in my head, on my temples. "Oh, yes, I care," she said slowly, "but that—that makes it all the worse. Why, yes, I care—yes, yes. It hurts me to see you. I might . . . It would draw me away. I have my allotted course. And you—— Don't you see, you would influence me; you would be—you *are*—a disease —for me."

"But," I said, "I could—I would—do anything."

I had only the faintest ideas of what I would do—for her sake.

"Ah, no," she said, "you must not say that. You don't understand . . . Even that would mean misery for you—and I—I could not bear. Don't you see? Even now, before you have done your allotted part, I am wanting—oh, wanting—to let you go . . . But I must not; I must not. You must go on . . . and bear it for a little while more—and then . . ."

There was a tension somewhere, a string somewhere that was stretched tight and vibrating. I was tremulous with an excitement that overmastered my powers of speech, that surpassed my understanding.

"Don't you see . . ." she asked again, "you are the past—the passing. We could never meet. You are . . . for me . . . only the portrait of a man—of a man who has been dead—oh, a long time; and I, for you, only a possibility . . . a conception

. . . You work to bring me on—to make me possible."

"But——" I said. The idea was so difficult to grasp. "I will—there must be a way——"

"No," she answered, "there is no way—you must go back; must try. There will be Churchill and what he stands for—He won't die, he won't even care much for losing this game . . . not much . . . And you will have to forget me. There is no other way—no bridge. We can't meet, you and I . . ."

The words goaded me to fury. I began to pace furiously up and down. I wanted to tell her that I would throw away everything for her, would crush myself out, would be a lifeless tool, would do anything. But I could tear no words out of the stone that seemed to surround me.

"You may even tell him, if you like, what I and Gurnard are going to do. It will make no difference; he will fall. But you would like him to—to make a good fight for it, wouldn't you? That is all I can do . . . for your sake."

I began to speak—as if I had not spoken for years. The house seemed to be coming to life; there were noises of opening doors, of voices outside.

"I believe you care enough," I said, "to give it all up for me. I believe you do, and I want you." I continued to pace up and down. The noises of returning day grew loud; frightfully loud. It was as if I must hasten, must get said what I had to say, as if I must raise my voice to make it heard amid the clamour of a world awakening to life.

"I believe you do . . . I believe you do . . ." I said again and again, "and I want you." My voice rose higher and higher. She stood motionless, an inscrutable white figure, like some silent Greek statue, a harmony of falling folds of heavy drapery perfectly motionless.

"I want you," I said—"I want you, I want you, I want you." It was unbearable to myself.

"Oh, be quiet," she said at last. "Be quiet! If you had wanted me I have been here. It is too late. All these days; all these——"

"But . . ." I said.

From without someone opened the great shutters of the windows, and the light from the outside world burst in upon us.

CHAPTER FIFTEEN

WE PARTED in London next day, I hardly know where. She seemed so part of my being, was for me so little more than an intellectual force, so little of a physical personality, that I cannot remember where my eyes lost sight of her.

I had desolately made the crossing from country to country, had convoyed my aunt to her big house in one of the gloomy squares in a certain district, and then we had parted. Even afterward it was as if she were still beside me, as if I had only to look round to find her eyes upon me. She remained the propelling force, I a boat thrust out upon a mill-pond, moving more and more slowly. I had been for so long in the shadow of that great house, shut in among the gloom, that all this light, this blazing world—it was a June day in London— seemed impossible, and hateful. Over there, there had been nothing but very slow, fading minutes; now there was a past, a future. It was as if I stood between them in a cleft of unscalable rocks.

I went about mechanically, made arrangements for my housing, moved in and out of rooms in the enormous mausoleum of a club that was all the home I had, in a sort of stupor. Suddenly I remembered that I had been thinking of something; that she had been talking of Churchill. I had had a letter from him on the morning of the day before. When I read it, Churchill and his *"Cromwell"* had risen in my mind like preposterous phantoms; the one as unreal as the other—as alien. I seemed to have passed an infinity of æons beyond them.

The one and the other belonged as absolutely to the past as a past year belongs. The thought of them did not bring with it the tremulously unpleasant sensations that, as a rule, come with the thoughts of a too recent *temps jadis*, but rather as a vein of rose across a gray evening. I had passed his letter over; had dropped it half-read among the litter of the others. Then there had seemed to be a haven into whose mouth I was drifting.

Now I should have to pick the letters up again, all of them; set to work desolately to pick up the threads of the past; and work it back into life as one does half-drowned things. I set about it listlessly. There remained of that time an errand for my aunt, an errand that would take me to Etchingham; something connected with her land steward. I think the old lady had ideas of inducting me into a position that it had grown tacitly acknowledged I was to fill. I was to go down there; to see about some alterations that were in progress; and to make arrangements for my aunt's return. I was so tired, so dog tired, and the day still had so many weary hours to run, that I recognised instinctively that if I were to come through it sane I must tire myself more, must keep on going—until I sank. I drifted down to Etchingham that evening. I sent a messenger over to Churchill's cottage, waited for an answer that told me that Churchill was there, and then slept, and slept.

I woke back in the world again, in a world that contained the land steward and the manor house. I had a sense of recovered power from the sight of them, of the sunlight on the stretches of turf, of the mellow, golden stonework of the long range of buildings, from the sound of a chime of bells that came wonderfully sweetly over the soft swelling of the close turf. The feeling came not from any sense of prospective ownership but from the acute consciousness of what these things stood for. I did not recognise it then, but later I understood; for the present it was enough to have again the power to set my foot on the ground, heel first. In the streets of the little town there was a sensation of holiday, not pronounced enough to call for flags, but enough to convey the idea of waiting for an event.

The land steward, at the end of a tour amongst cottages, explained there was to be a celebration in the neighbourhood—a "cock-and-hen show with a political annex"; the latter under the auspices of Miss Churchill. Churchill himself was to speak; there was a possibility of a pronouncement. I found London reporters at my inn, men I half knew. They expressed mitigated delight at the view of me, and over a lunch-table let me know what "one said"—what one said of the outside of events I knew too well internally. They most of them had the air of my aunt's solicitor when he had said, "Even I did not realise . . ." their positions saving them the necessity of concealing surprise. "One can't know *everything*." They fumbled amusingly about the causes, differed with one another, but were surprisingly unanimous as to effects, as to the panic and the call for purification. It was rather extraordinary, too, how large de Mersch loomed on the horizon over here. It was as if the whole world centred in him, as if he represented the modern spirit that must be purified away by burning before things could return to their normal state. I knew what he represented . . . but there it was.

It was part of my programme, the attendance at the poultry show; I was to go back to the cottage with Churchill, after he had made his speech. It was rather extraordinary, the sensations of that function. I went in rather late, with the reporter of the *Hour*, who was anxious to do me the favour of introducing me without payment—it was his way of making himself pleasant, and I had the reputation of knowing celebrities. It *was* rather extraordinary to be back again in the midst of this sort of thing, to be walking over a crowded, green paddock, hedged in with tall trees and dotted here and there with the gaily striped species of tent that is called marquee. And the type of face, and the style of the costume! They would have seemed impossible the day before yesterday.

There were all Miss Churchill's gang of great dames, muslin rustling, marriageable daughters, a continual twitter of voices, and a sprinkling of the peasantry, dun-coloured and struck speechless.

One of the great ladies surveyed me as I stood in the centre of an open space, surveyed me through tortoise-shell glasses on the end of a long handle, and beckoned me to her side.

"You are unattached?" she asked. She had pretensions to voice the county, just as my aunt undoubtedly set the tone of its doings, decided who was visitable, and just as Miss Churchill gave the political tone. "You may wait upon me, then," she said; "my daughter is with her young man. That is the correct phrase, is it not?"

She was a great lady, who stood nearly six foot high, and whom one would have styled buxom, had one dared. "I have a grievance," she went on; "I must talk to someone. Come this way. *There!*" She pointed with the handle of her glasses to a pen of glossy black birds. "You see! . . . Not even commended!— and I assure you the trouble I have taken over them, with the idea of setting an example to the tenantry, is incredible. They give a prize to one of our own tenants

. . . which is as much as telling the man that he is an example to *me*. Then they wonder that the country is going to the dogs. I assure you that after breakfast I have had the scraps collected from the plates—that was the course recommended by the poultry manuals—and have taken them out with my own hands."

The sort of thing passed for humour in the county, and, being delivered with an air and a half Irish ruefulness, passed well enough.

"And that reminds me," she went on, "—I mean the fact that the country is going to the dogs, as my husband (You haven't seen him anywhere, have you? He is one of the judges, and I want to have a word with him about my Orpingtons) says every morning after he has looked at his paper—that . . . oh, that you have been in Paris, haven't you? with your aunt. Then, of course, you have seen this famous Duc de Mersch?"

She looked at me humorously through her glasses. "I'm going to pump you, you know," she said, "it is the duty that is expected of me. I have to talk for a countyful of women without a tongue in their heads. So tell me about him. Is it true that he is at the bottom of all this mischief? Is it through him that this man committed suicide? They say so. He *was* mixed up in that Royalist plot, wasn't he?—and the people that have been failing all over the place *are* mixed up with him, aren't they?"

"I . . . I really don't know," I said; "if you say so . . ."

"Oh, I assure you I'm sound enough," she answered; "the Churchills—I know you're a friend of his—haven't a stauncher ally than I am, and I should only be too glad to be able to contradict. But it's so difficult. I assure you I go out of my way; talk to the most outrageous people, deny the very possibility of Mr. Churchill's being in any way implicated. One knows that it's impossible, but what can one do? I have said again and again—to people like grocers' wives; even to the grocers, for that matter—that Mr. Churchill is a states-man, and that if he insists that this odious man's rail-way must go through, it is in the interests of the country that it should. I tell them . . ."

She paused for a minute to take breath and then went on: "I was speaking to a man of that class only this morning, rather an intelligent man and quite nice—I was saying, 'Don't you see, my dear Mr. Tull, that it is a question of international politics? If the grand duke does not get the money for his railway, the grand duke will be turned out of his—what is it—principality? And that would be most dangerous—in the present con-dition of affairs over there, and besides . . .' The man listened very respectfully, but I could see that he was not convinced. I buckled to again . . .

"'And besides,' I said, 'there is the question of Greenland itself. We English must have Greenland . . . sooner or later. It touches you, even. You have a son who's above—who doesn't care for life in a country town, and you want to send him abroad—with a little capital. Well, Greenland is just the place for him.' The man looked at me, and almost shook his head in my face.

"'If you'll excuse me, my lady,' he said, 'it won't do. Mr. Churchill is a man above hocus-pocus. Well I know it that have had dealings with him. But . . . well, the long and the short of it is, my lady, that you can't touch pitch and not be defiled; or, leastwise, people'll think you've been defiled—those that don't know you. The foreign nations are all very well, and the grand duchy—and the getting hold of Greenland, but what touches me is this—My neighbour Slingsby had a little money, and he gets a prospectus.   It looked very well—very well—and he brings it in to me.   I did not have anything to do with it, but Slingsby did. Well, now there's Slingsby on the rates and his wife a lady born, almost.   I might have been taken in the same way but for—for the grace of God, I'm minded to say.   Well, Slingsby's a good man, and used to be a hard-working man—all his life, and now it turns out that that prospectus came about by the man de Mersch's manœuvres—"wild-cat schemes," they call them in the paper that I read.   And there's any number of them started by de Mersch or his agents.   Just for what? That de Mersch may be the richest man in the world and a philanthropist.   Well, then, where's Slingsby, if that's philanthropy?   So Mr. Churchill comes along and says, in a manner of speaking, "That's all very well, but this same Mr. Mersch is the grand duke of somewhere or other, and we must bolster him up in his kingdom, or else there will be trouble with the powers."   Powers— what's powers to me?—or Greenland? when there's Slingsby, a man I've smoked a pipe with every market evening of my life, in the workhouse?   And there's hundreds of Slingsbys all over the country.'

"The man was working himself—Slingsby *was* a good sort of man.   It shocked even me.   One knows what goes on in one's own village, of course.   And it's only too true that there's hundreds of Slingsbys—I'm not boring you, am I?"

I did not answer for a moment.   "I—I had no idea," I said; "I have been so long out of it and over there one did not realise the   . . .   the feeling."

"You've been well out of it," she answered; "one has had to suffer, I assure you."   I believed that she had had to suffer; it must have taken a good deal to make that lady complain.   Her large, ruddy features followed the droop of her eyes down to the fringe of the parasol that she was touching the turf with. We were sitting on garden seats in the dappled shade of enormous elms.

There was in the air a touch of the sounds discoursed by a yeomanry band at the other end of the grounds. One could see the red of their uniforms through moving rifts in the crowd of white dresses.

"That wasn't even the worst," she said suddenly, lifting her eyes and looking away between the trunks of the trees. "The man has been reading the papers and he gave me the benefit of his reflections. 'Some-one's got to be punished for this,' he said; 'we've got to show them that you can't be hand-and-glove with that sort of blackguard without paying for it. I don't say, mind you, that Mr. Churchill is or ever has been. I know him, and I trust him. But there's more than me in the world, and they can't all know him. Well, here's the papers saying—or they don't say it, but they hint, which is worse in a way—that he must be, or he wouldn't stick up for the man. They say the man's a blackguard out and out—in Greenland too; has the blacks mur-dered. Churchill says the blacks are to be safe-guarded, that's the word. Well, they may be—but so ought Slingsby to have been, yet it didn't help him. No, my lady, we've got to put our own house in order and that first, before thinking of the powers or places like Green-land. What's the good of the saner policy that Mr. Churchill talks about, if you can't trust any one with your money, and have to live on the capital? If you can't sleep at night for thinking that you may be in the workhouse to-morrow—like Slingsby? The first duty of men in Mr. Churchill's position—as I see it—is to see that we're able to be confident of honest dealing. That's what we want, not Greenlands. That's how we all feel, and you know it, too, or else you, a great lady, wouldn't stop to talk to a man like me. And, mind you, I'm true blue, always have been and always shall be, and, if it was a matter of votes, I'd give mine to Mr. Churchill to-morrow. But there's a many that wouldn't, *and* there's a many that believe the hintings.'"

My lady stopped and sighed from a broad bosom. "What could I say?" she went on again. "I know Mr. Churchill and I like him—and everyone that knows him likes him. I'm one of the stalwarts, mind you; I'm not for giving in to popular clamour; I'm for the 'saner policy,' like Churchill. But, as the man said: 'There's a many that believe the hintings.' And I almost wish Churchill . . . However, you understand what I meant when I said that one had had to suffer."

"Oh, I understand," I said. I was beginning to. "And Churchill?" I asked later, "he gives no sign of relenting?"

"Would you have him?" she asked sharply; "would you make him if you could?" She had an air of challenging. "I'm for the 'saner policy,' cost what it may. He owes it to himself to sacrifice himself, if it comes to that."

"I'm with you too," I answered, "over boot and spur." Her enthusiasm was contagious, and unnecessary.

"Oh, he'll stick," she began again after consultation with the parasol fringe. "You'll hear him after a minute. It's a field day to-day. You'll miss the other heavy guns if you stop with me. I do it ostentatiously —wait until they've done. They're all trembling; all of them. My husband will be on the platform—trembling too. He is a type of them. All day long and at odd moments at night I talk to him—out-talk him and silence him. What's the state of popular feeling to him? (He's for the country, not the town—this sort of thing has nothing to do with him. It's a matter to be settled by Jews in the City. Well, he sees it at night, and then in the morning the papers undo all my work. He begins to talk about his seat—which *I* got for him. I've been the 'voice of the county' for years now. Well, it'll soon be a voice without a county . . . What is it? 'The old order changeth.' So, I've arranged it that I shall wait until the trembling big-wigs have stuttered their speeches out, and then I'm going to sail down the centre aisle and listen to Churchill with visible signs of approval. It won't do much to-day, but there was a time when it would have changed the course of an election . . . Ah, there's Effie's young man. It's time."

She rose and marched, with the air of going to a last sacrifice, across the deserted sward toward a young man who was passing under the calico flag of the gateway.

"It's all right, Willoughby," she said, as we drew level, "I've found someone else to face the music with me; you can go back to Effie." A bronzed and grateful young man murmured thanks to me.

"It's an awful relief, Granger," he said; "can't think how you can do it. I'm hooked, but you . . ."

"He's the better man," his mother-in-law-elect said, over her shoulder. She sailed slowly up the aisle beside me, an almost heroic figure of a matron. "Splendidly timed, you see," she said, "do you observe my husband's embarrassment?"

It was splendid to see Churchill again, standing there negligently, with the diffidence of a boy amid the bustle of applause. I understood suddenly why I loved him so, this tall, gray man with the delicate, almost grotesque, mannerisms. He appealed to me by sheer force of picturesqueness, appealed as some forgotten mediæval city might. I was concerned for him as for some such dying place, standing above the level plains; I was jealous lest it should lose one jot of its glory, of its renown. He advocated his saner policy before all those people; stood up there and spoke gently, persuasively, without any stress of emotion, without more movement than an occasional flutter of the glasses he held in his hand. One would never have recognised that the thing was a fighting speech but for the occasional shiver of his audience. They were thinking of their Slingsbys; he affecting, insouciantly, to treat them as rational people.

It was extraordinary to sit there shut in by that wall of people all of one type, of one idea; the idea of getting back; all conscious that a force of which they knew nothing was dragging them forward over the edge of a glacier, into a crevasse. They wanted to get back, were struggling, panting even—as a nation pants—to get back by their own way that they understood and saw; were hauling, and hauling desperately, at the weighted rope that was dragging them forward. Churchill stood up there and repeated: "Mine is the only way—the saner policy," and his words would fly all over the country to fall upon the deaf ears of the panic-stricken, who could not understand the use of calmness, of trifling even, in the face of danger, who suspected the calmness as one suspects the thing one has not. At the end of it I received his summons to a small door at the back of the building. The speech seemed to have passed out of his mind far more than out of mine.

"So you have come," he said; "that's good, and so . . . Let us walk a little way . . . out of this. My aunt will pick us up on the road." He linked his arm into mine and propelled me swiftly down the bright, broad street. "I'm sorry you came in for that, but— one has to do these things."

There was a sort of resisted numbness in his voice, a lack of any resiliency. My heart sank a little It was as if I were beside an invalid who did not—must not —know his condition; as if I were pledged not to notice anything. In the open the change struck home as a hammer strikes; in the pitiless searching of the unrestrained light, his grayness, his tremulousness, his aloofness from the things about him, came home to me like a pang.

"You look a bit fagged," I said, "perhaps we ought not to talk about work." His thoughts seemed to come back from a great distance, oh, from an infinite distance beyond the horizon, the soft hills of that fat country. "You want rest," I added.

"I—oh, no," he answered, "I can't have it . . . till the end of the session. I'm used to it too."

He began talking briskly about the "Cromwell;" proofs had emerged from the infinite and wanted attention. There were innumerable little matters, things to be copied for the appendix and revisions. It was impossible for me to keep my mind upon them.

It had come suddenly home to me that this was the world that I belonged to; that I had come back to it as if from an underworld; that to this I owed allegiance. She herself had recognised that; she herself had bidden me tell him what was a-gate against him. It was a duty too; he was my friend. But, face to face with him, it became almost an impossibility. It was impossible even to put it into words. The mere ideas seemed to be untranslatable, to savour of madness. I found myself in the very position that she had occupied at the commencement of our relations: that of having to explain—say, to a Persian—the working principles of the telegraph. And I was not equal to the task. At the same time I had to do something. I had to. It would be abominable to have to go through life forever, alone with the consciousness of that sort of treachery of silence. But how could I tell him even the comprehensibles? What kind of sentence was I to open with? With pluckings of an apologetic string, without prelude at all—or how? I grew conscious that there was need for haste; he was looking behind him down the long white road for the carriage that was to pick us up.

"My dear fellow . . ." I began. He must have noted a change in my tone, and looked at me with suddenly lifted eyebrows. "You know my sister is going to marry Mr. Gurnard."

"Why, no," he answered—"that is . . . I've heard . . ." He began to offer good wishes.

"No, no," I interrupted him hurriedly, "not that. But I happen to know that Gurnard is meditating . . . is going to separate from you in public matters." An expression of dismay spread over his face.

"My dear fellow," he began.

"Oh, I'm not drunk," I said bitterly, "but I've been behind the scenes—for a long time. And I could not . . . couldn't let the thing go on without a word." He stopped in the road and looked at me.

"Yes, yes," he said, "I daresay . . . But what does it lead to? . . . Even if I could listen to you —I can't go behind the scenes. Mr. Gurnard may differ from me in points, but don't you see? . . ." He had walked on slowly, but he came to a halt again. "We had better put these matters out of our minds. Of course you are not drunk; but one is tied down in these matters . . ."

He spoke very gently, as if he did not wish to offend me by this closing of the door. He seemed suddenly to grow very old and very gray. There was a stile in the dusty hedge-row, and he walked toward it, meditating. In a moment he looked back at me. "I had forgotten," he said; "I meant to suggest that we should wait here—I am a little tired." He perched himself on the top bar and became lost in the inspection of the cord of his glasses. I went toward him.

"I knew," I said, "that you could not listen to . . . to the sort of thing. But there were reasons. I felt forced. You will forgive me." He looked up at me, starting as if he had forgotten my presence.

"Yes, yes," he said, "I have a certain—I can't think of the right word—say respect—for your judgment and —and motives . . . but you see, there are, for instance, my colleagues. I couldn't go to them . . ." He lost the thread of his idea.

"To tell the truth," I said, with a sudden impulse for candour, "it isn't the political aspect of the matter, but the personal. I spoke because it was just possible that I might be of service to you—personally—and because I would like you . . . to make a good fight for it." I had borrowed her own words.

He looked up at me and smiled. "Thank you," he said. "I believe you think it's a losing game," he added, with a touch of gray humour that was like a genial hour of sunlight on a wintry day. I did not answer. A little way down the road Miss Churchill's carriage whirled into sight, sparkling in the sunlight, and sending up an attendant cloud of dust that melted like smoke through the dog-roses of the leeward hedge.

"So you don't think much of me as a politician," Churchill suddenly deduced smilingly. "You had better not tell that to my aunt."

I went up to town with Churchill that evening. There was nothing waiting for me there, but I did not want to think. I wanted to be among men, among crowds of men, to be dazed, to be stupefied, to hear nothing for the din of life, to be blinded by the blaze of lights.

There were plenty of people in Churchill's carriage; a military member and a local member happened to be in my immediate neighbourhood. Their minds were full of the financial scandals, and they dinned their alternating opinions into me. I assured them that I knew nothing about the matter, and they grew more solicitous for my enlightenment.

"It all comes from having too many eggs in one basket," the local member summed up. "The old-fashioned small enterprises had their disadvantages, but —mind you—these gigantic trusts . . . Isn't that so, General?"

"Oh, I quite agree with you," the general barked; "at the same time . . ." Their voices sounded on, intermingling, indistinguishable, soothing even. I seemed to be listening to the hum of a threshing-machine —a passage of sound booming on one note, a passage, a half-tone higher, and so on, and so on. Visible things grew hazy, fused into one another.

CHAPTER SIXTEEN

WE REACHED London somewhat late in the evening—
in the twilight of a summer day. There was the hurry
and bustle of arrival, a hurry and bustle that changed
the tenor of my thoughts and broke their train. As I
stood reflecting before the door of the carriage, I felt a
friendly pressure of a hand on my shoulder.

"You'll see to that," Churchill's voice said in my ear.
"You'll set the copyists to work."

"I'll go to the Museum to-morrow," I said. There
were certain extracts to be made for the "Life of
Cromwell"—extracts from pamphlets that we had not
conveniently at disposal. He nodded, walked swiftly
toward his brougham, opened the door and entered.

I remember so well that last sight of him—of his long,
slim figure bending down for the entrance, woefully
solitary, woefully weighted; remember so well the gleam
of the carriage panels reflecting the murky light of the
bare London terminus, the attitude of the coachman
stiffly reining back the horse; the thin hand that reached
out, a gleam of white, to turn the gleaming handle.
There was something intimately suggestive of the man
in the motion of that hand, in its tentative outstretch-
ing, its gentle, half-persuasive—almost theoretic—
grasp of the handle. The pleasure of its friendly pressure on my shoulder carried me over some minutes of
solitude, its weight on my body removing another from
my mind. I had feared that my ineffective disclosure
had chilled what of regard he had for me. He had said
nothing, his manner had said nothing, but I had feared.

In the railway carriage he had sat remote from me, buried in papers. But that touch on my shoulder was enough to set me well with myself again, if not to afford scope for pleasant improvisation. It at least showed me that he bore me no ill-will, otherwise he would hardly have touched me. Perhaps, even, he was grateful to me, not for service, but for ineffectual good-will. Whatever I read into it, that was the last time he spoke to me, and the last time he touched me. And I loved him very well. Things went so quickly after that.

In a moderately cheerful frame of mind I strolled the few yards that separated me from my club—intent on dining. In my averseness to solitude I sat down at a table where sat already a little, bald-headed, false-toothed Anglo-Indian, a man who bored me into fits of nervous excitement. He was by way of being an incredibly distant uncle of my own. As a rule I avoided him, to-night I dined with him. He was a person of interminable and incredibly inaccurate reminiscences. His long residence in an indigo-producing swamp had affected his memory, which was supported by only very occasional visits to England.

He told me tales of my poor father and of my poor, dear mother, and of Mr. Bromptons and Mrs. Kenwards who had figured on their visiting lists away back in the musty sixties.

"Your poor, dear father was precious badly off then," he said; "he had a hard struggle for it. I had a bad time of it too; worm had got at all my plantations, so I couldn't help him, poor chap. I think, mind you, Kenny Granger treated him very badly. He might have done something for him—he had influence, Kenny had."

Kenny was my uncle, the head of the family, the husband of my aunt.

"They weren't on terms," I said.

"Oh, I know, I know," the old man mumbled, "but still, for one's only brother . . . However, you contrive to do yourselves pretty well. You're making your pile, aren't you? Someone said to me the other day—can't remember who it was—that you were quite one of the rising men—quite one of *the* men."

"Very kind of someone," I said.

"And now I see," he went on, lifting up a copy of a morning paper, over which I had found him munching his salmon cutlet, "now I see your sister is going to marry a cabinet minister. Ah!" he shook his poor, muddled, baked head, "I remember you both as tiny little dots."

"Why," I said, "she can hardly have been born then."

"Oh, yes," he affirmed, "that was when I came over in '78. She remembered, too, that I brought her over an ivory doll—she remembered."

"You have seen her?" I asked.

"Oh, I called two or three weeks—no, months—ago. She's the image of your poor, dear mother," he added, "at that age; I remarked upon it to your aunt, but, of course, she could not remember. They were not married until after the quarrel."

A sudden restlessness made me bolt the rest of my tepid dinner. With my return to the upper world, and the return to me of a will, despair of a sort had come back. I had before me the problem—the necessity—of winning her. Once I was out of contact with her she grew smaller, less of an idea, more of a person—that one could win. And there were two ways. I must either woo her as one woos a person barred; must compel her to take flight, to abandon, to cast away everything; or I must go to her as an eligible suitor with the Etchingham acres and possibilities of a future on that basis. This fantastic old man with his mumbled reminiscences spoilt me for the last. One remembers sooner or later that a county-man may not marry his reputed sister without scandal. And I craved her intensely.

She had upon me the effect of an incredible stimulant; away from her I was like a drunkard cut off from his liquor; an opium-taker from his drug. I hardly existed; I hardly thought.

I had an errand at my aunt's house; had a message to deliver, sympathetic enquiries to make—and I wanted to see her, to gain some sort of information from her; to spy out the land; to ask her for terms. There was a change in the appearance of the house, an adventitious brightness that indicated the rise in the fortunes of the family. For me the house was empty and the great door closed hollowly behind me. My sister was not at home. It seemed abominable to me that she should be out; that she could be talking to any one, or could exist without me. I went sullenly across the road to the palings of the square. As I turned the corner I found my head pivoting on my neck. I was looking over my shoulder at the face of the house, was wondering which was her window.

"Like a love-sick boy—like a damn love-sick boy," I growled at myself. My sense of humour was returning to me. There began a pilgrimage in search of companionship.

London was a desert more solitary than was believable. On those brilliant summer evenings the streets were crowded, were alive, bustled with the clatter of footsteps, with the chitter-chatter of voices, of laughter.

It was impossible to walk, impossible to do more than tread on one's own toes; one was almost blinded by the constant passing of faces. It was like being in a wheat-field with one's eyes on a level with the indistinguishable ears. One was alone in one's intense contempt for all these faces, all these contented faces; one towered intellectually above them; one towered into regions of rarefaction. And down below they enjoyed themselves. One understood life better; they better how to live. That struck me then—in Oxford Street. There was the intense good-humour, the absolute disregard of the minor inconveniences, of the inconveniences of a crowd, of the ignominy of being one of a crowd. There was the intense poetry of the soft light, the poetry of the summer-night coolness, and they understood how to enjoy it. I turned up an ancient court near Bedford Row.

"In the name of God," I said, "I will enjoy . . ." and I did. The poetry of those old deserted quarters came suddenly home to me—all the little commonplace thoughts; all the commonplace associations of Georgian London. For the time I was done with the meanings of things.

I was seeking Lea—he was not at home. The quarter was honeycombed with the homes of people one knows; of people one used to know, excellent young men who wrote for the papers, who sub-edited papers, who designed posters, who were always just the same. One forgot them for a year or two, one came across them again and found them just the same—still writing for the same papers, still sub-editing the same papers, designing the same posters. I was in the mood to rediscover them in the privacies of their hearths, with the same excellent wives making fair copies of the same manuscripts, with the same gaiety of the same indifferent whiskey, brown or pale or suspicious-looking, in heavy, square, cut-glass stoppered decanters, and with the same indifferent Virginian tobacco at the same level in the same jars.

I was in the mood for this stability, for the excellent household article that was their view of life and literature. I wanted to see it again, to hear again how it was filling the unvarying, allotted columns of the daily, the weekly, or the monthly journals. I wanted to breathe again this mild atmosphere where there are no longer hopes or fears. But, alas! . . .

I rang bell after bell of that gloomy central London district. You know what happens. One pulls the knob under the name of the person one seeks—pulls it three, or, it may be, four times in vain. One rings the housekeeper's bell; it reverberates, growing fainter and fainter, gradually stifled by a cavernous subterranean atmosphere. After an age a head peeps round the opening door, the head of a hopeless anachronism, the head of a widow of early Victorian merit, or of an orphan of incredible age. One asks for So-and-so—he's out; for Williams—he's expecting an increase of family, and has gone into the country with madame. And Waring? Oh, he's gone no one knows where, and Johnson who used to live at Number 44 only comes up to town on Tuesdays now. I exhausted the possibilities of that part of Bloomsbury, the possibilities of variety in the types of housekeepers. The rest of London divided itself into bands—into zones. Between here and Kensington the people that I knew could not be called on after dinner, those who lived at Chiswick and beyond were hyperborean—one was bound by the exigencies of time. It was ten o'clock as I stood reflecting on a doorstep—on Johnson's doorstep. I must see somebody, must talk to somebody, before I went to bed in the cheerless room at the club. It was true I might find a political stalwart in the smoking-room—

but that was a last resort, a desperate and ignominious *pis aller*.

There was Fox, I should find him at the office. But it needed a change of tone before I could contemplate with equanimity the meeting of that individual. I had been preparing myself to confront all the ethically excellent young men and Fox was, ethically speaking, far from excellent, middle-aged, rubicund, leery—a free lance of genius. I made the necessary change in my tone of mind and ran him to earth.

The Watteau room was further enlivened by the introduction of a scarlet plush couch of sumptuous design. By its side stood a couple of electric lights. The virulent green of their shades made the colours of the be-shepherded wall-panels appear almost unearthly, and threw impossible shadows on the deal partition. Round the couch stood chairs with piles of papers neatly arranged on them; round it, on the floor, were more papers lying like the leaves of autumn that one sings of. On it lay Fox, enveloped in a Shetland shawl—a good shawl that was the only honest piece of workmanship in the tom-tawdry place. Fox was as rubicund as ever, but his features were noticeably peaked and there were heavy lines under his eyes—lines cast into deep shadow by the light by which he was reading. I entered unannounced, and was greeted by an indifferent upward glance that changed into one of something like pleasure as he made out my features in the dim light.

"Hullo, you old country hawbuck," he said, with spasmodic jocularity; "I'm uncommon glad to see you." He came to a jerky close, with an indrawing of his breath. "I'm about done," he went on. "Same old thing—sciatica. Took me just after I got here this afternoon; sent out one of the messengers to buy me a sofa, and here I've been ever since. Well, and what's brought you up—don't answer, I know all about it. I've got to keep on talking until this particular spasm's over, or else I shall scream and disturb the flow of Soane's leader. Well, and now you've come, you'll stop and help me to put the *Hour* to bed, won't you? And then you can come and put me to bed."

He went on talking at high pressure, exaggerating his expressions, heightening his humorous touches with punctuations of rather wild laughter. At last he came to a stop with a half suppressed "Ah!" and a long in-drawing of the breath.

"That's over," he said. "Give me a drop of brandy —there's a good fellow." I gave him his nip. Then I explained to him that I couldn't work for the *Hour;* that I wasn't on terms with de Mersch.

"Been dropping money over him?" he asked, cheer-fully. I explained a little more—that there was a lady.

"Oh, it's *that*," Fox said. "The man *is* a fool . . . But anyhow Mersch don't count for much in this par-ticular show. He's no money in it even, so you may put your pride in your pocket, or wherever you keep it. It's all right. Straight. He's only the small change."

"But," I said, "everyone says; you said your-self . . ."

"To be sure," he answered. "But you don't think that *I* play second fiddle to a bounder of that calibre. Not really?"

He looked at me with a certain seriousness. I re-membered, as I had remembered once before, that Fox was a personality—a power. I had never realized till then how entirely—fundamentally—different he was from any other man that I knew. He was surprising enough to have belonged to another race. He looked at me, not as if he cared whether I gave him his due or no, but as if he were astonished at my want of perception of the fact. He let his towzled head fall back upon the plush cushions. "You might kick him from here to Greenland for me," he said; "I wouldn't weep. It suits me to hold him up, and a kicking might restore his equilibrium. I'm sick of him—I've told him so. I knew there *was* a woman. But don't you worry; *I'm* the man here."

"If that's the case . . ." I said.

"Oh, that's it," he answered.

I helped him to put the paper to bed; took some of the work off his hands. It was all part of the getting back to life; of the resuming of rusty armour; and I wanted to pass the night. I was not unused to it, as it happened. Fox had had several of these fits during my year, and during most of them I had helped him through the night; once or twice for three on end. Once I had had entire control for a matter of five nights. But they gave me a new idea of Fox, those two or three weird hours that night. It was as if I had never seen him before. The attacks grew more virulent as the night advanced. He groaned and raved, and said things—oh, the most astounding things in gibberish that upset one's nerves and everything else. At the height he sang hymns and then, as the fits passed, relapsed into incredible clear-headedness. It gave me, I say, a new idea of Fox. It was as if, for all the time I had known him, he had been playing a part, and that only now, in the delirium of his pain, in the madness into which he drank himself, were fragments of the real man thrown to the surface. I grew, at last, almost afraid to be alone with him in the dead small hours of the morning, and longed for the time when I could go to bed among the uninspiring, marble-topped furniture of my club.

CHAPTER SEVENTEEN

AT NOON of the next day I gave Fox a look-in at his own flat. He was stretched upon a sofa—it was evident that I was to take such of his duties as were takeable. He greeted me with words to that effect.

"Don't go filling the paper with your unbreeched geniuses," he said, genially, "and don't overwork yourself. There's really nothing to do, but your being there will keep that little beast Evans from getting too cock-a-hoop. He'd like to jerk me out altogether; thinks they'd get on just as well without me."

I expressed in my manner general contempt for Evans, and was taking my leave.

"Oh, and——" Fox called after me. I turned back. "The Greenland mail ought to be in to-day. If Callan's contrived to get his flood-gates open, run his stuff in, there's a good chap. It's a feature and all that, you know."

"I suppose Soane's to have a look at it?" I asked.

"Oh, yes," he answered; "but tell him to keep strictly to old Cal's lines—rub that into him. If he were to get drunk and run in some of his own tips it'd be awkward. People are expecting Cal's stuff. Tell you what: you take him out to lunch, eh? Keep an eye on the supplies, and ram it into him that he's got to stick to Cal's line of argument."

"Soane's as bad as ever, then?" I asked.

"Oh," Fox answered, "he'll be all right for the stuff if you get that one idea into him." A prolonged and

179

acute fit of pain seized him. I fetched his man and left him to his rest.

At the office of the *Hour* I was greeted by the handing to me of a proof of Callan's manuscript. Evans, the man across the screen, was the immediate agent.

"I suppose it's got to go in, so I had it set up," he said.

"Oh, of course it's got to go in," I answered. "It's to go to Soane first, though."

"Soane's not here yet," he answered. I noted the tone of sub-acid pleasure in his voice. Evans would have enjoyed a fiasco.

"Oh, well," I answered, nonchalantly, "there's plenty of time. You allow space on those lines. I'll send round to hunt Soane up."

I felt called to be upon my mettle. I didn't much care about the paper, but I had a definite antipathy to being done by Evans—by a mad Welshman in a stubborn fit. I knew what was going to happen; knew that Evans would feign inconceivable stupidity, the sort of black stupidity that is at command of individuals of his primitive race. I was in for a day of petty worries. In the circumstances it was a thing to be thankful for; it dragged my mind away from larger issues. One has no time for brooding when one is driving a horse in a jibbing fit.

Evans was grimly conscious that I was moderately ignorant of technical details; he kept them well before my eyes all day long.

At odd moments I tried to read Callan's article. It was impossible. It opened with a description of the squalor of the Greenlander's life, and contained tawdry passages of local colour.

I knew what was coming. This was the view of the Greenlanders of pre-Merschian Greenland, elaborated, after the manner of Callan—the Special Commissioner —so as to bring out the glory and virtue of the work of regeneration. Then in a gush of superlatives the work itself would be described. I knew quite well what was coming, and was temperamentally unable to read more than the first ten lines.

Everything was going wrong. The printers developed one of their sudden crazes for asking idiotic questions. Their messengers came to Evans, Evans sent them round the pitch-pine screen to me. "Mr. Jackson wants to know——"

The fourth of the messengers that I had despatched to Soane returned with the news that Soane would arrive at half-past nine. I sent out in search of the strongest coffee that the city afforded. Soane arrived. He had been ill, he said, very ill. He desired to be fortified with champagne. I produced the coffee.

Soane was the son of an Irish peer. He had magnificent features—a little blurred nowadays—and a remainder of the grand manner. His nose was a marvel of classic workmanship, but the floods of time had reddened and speckled it—not offensively but ironically; his hair was turning gray, his eyes were bloodshot, his heavy moustache rather ragged. He inspired one with the respect that one feels for a man who has lived and does not care a curse. He had a weird intermittent genius that made it worth Fox's while to put up with his lapses and his brutal snubs.

I produced the coffee and pointed to the sofa of the night before.

"Damn it," he said, "I'm ill, I tell you; I want . . ."

"Exactly!" I cut in. "You want a rest, old fellow. Here's Cal's article. We want something special about it. If you don't feel up to it I'll send round to Jenkins."

"Damn Jenkins," he said; "I'm up to it."

"You understand," I said, "you're to write strictly on Callan's lines. Don't insert any information from extraneous sources. And make it as slashing as you like—on those lines."

He grunted in acquiescence. I left him lying on the sofa, drinking the coffee. I had tenderly arranged the lights for him as Fox had arranged them the night before. As I went out to get my dinner I was comfortably aware of him, holding the slips close to his muddled eyes and philosophically damning the nature of things.

When I returned, Soane, from his sofa, said something that I did not catch—something about Callan and his article.

"Oh, for God's sake," I answered, "don't worry me. Have some more coffee and stick to Cal's line of argument. That's what Fox said. I'm not responsible."

"Deuced queer," Soane muttered. He began to scribble with a pencil. From the tone of his voice I knew that he had reached the precise stage at which something brilliant—the real thing of its kind—might be expected.

Very late Soane finished his leader. He looked up as he wrote the last word.

"I've got it written," he said. "But . . . I say, what the deuce is up?   It's like being a tall clock with the mainspring breaking, this."

I rang the bell for someone to take the copy down.

"Your metaphor's too much for me, Soane," I said.

"It's appropriate all the way along," he maintained, "if you call me a mainspring. I've been wound up and wound up to write old de Mersch and his Greenland up —and it's been a tight wind, these days, I tell you. Then all of a sudden . . ."

A boy appeared and carried off the copy.

"All of a sudden," Soane resumed, "something gives—I suppose something's given—and there's a whirr-rr-rr and the hands fly backwards and old de Mersch and Greenland bump to the bottom, like the weights."

The boom of the great presses was rattling the window frames. Soane got up and walked toward one of the cupboards.

"Dry work," he said; "but the simile's just, isn't it?"

I gave one swift step toward the bell-button beside the desk. The proof of Callan's article, from which Soane had been writing, lay a crumpled white streamer on the brown wood of Fox's desk. I made toward it. As I stretched out my hand the solution slipped into my mind, coming with no more noise than that of a bullet; impinging with all the shock and remaining with all the pain. I had remembered the morning, over there in Paris, when she had told me that she had invited one of de Mersch's lieutenants to betray him by not concealing from Callan the real horrors of the Système Groënlandais—flogged, butchered, miserable natives, the famines, the vices, diseases, and the crimes. There came suddenly before my eyes the tall narrow room in my aunt's house, the opening of the door and her entry, followed by that of the woebegone governor of a province—the man who was to show Callan things—with his grating "*C'est entendu* . . ."

I remembered the scene distinctly; her words; her looks; my utter unbelief. I remembered too, that it had not saved me from a momentary sense of revolt against that inflexible intention of a treachery which was to be another step toward the inheritance of the earth. I had rejected the very idea, and here it had come; it was confronting me with all its meaning and

consequences. Callan *had* been shown things he had
not been meant to see, and had written the truth as he
had seen it. His article was a small thing in itself, but
he had been sent out there with tremendous flourishes
of de Mersch's trumpets. He was *the* man who could
be believed. De Mersch's supporters had practically
said: "If he condemns us we are indeed damned."
And now that the condemnation had come, it meant
ruin, as it seemed to me, for everybody I had known,
worked for, seen or heard of, during the last year of
my life. It was ruin for Fox, for Churchill, for the
ministers, and for the men who talk in railway carri-
ages, for shopkeepers and for the Government; it was a
menace to the institutions which hold us to the past,
that are our guarantees for the future. The safety of
everything one respected and believed in was involved
in the disclosure of an atrocious fraud, and the disclosure was in my hands. For that night I had the
power of the press in my keeping. People were waiting
for this pronouncement. De Mersch's last card was
his philanthropy; his model state and his happy
natives.

The drone of the presses made the floor under my
feet quiver, and the whole building vibrated as if the
earth itself had trembled. I was alone with my knowledge. Did she know; had she put the power in my
hand? But I was alone, and I was free.

I took up the proof and began to read, slanting the
page to the fall of the light. It was a phrenetic indictment, but under the paltry rhetoric of the man
there was genuine indignation and pain. There were
revolting details of cruelty to the miserable, helpless,
and defenceless; there were greed, and self-seeking,
stripped naked; but more revolting to see without a
mask was that falsehood which had been hiding under

the words that for ages had spurred men to noble deeds, to self-sacrifice, to heroism. What was appalling was the sudden perception that all the traditional ideals of honour, glory, conscience, had been committed to the upholding of a gigantic and atrocious fraud. The false-hood had spread stealthily, had eaten into the very heart of creeds and convictions that we lean upon in our passages between the past and the future. The old order of things had to live or perish with a lie. I saw all this with the intensity and clearness of a revelation; I saw it as though I had been asleep through a year of work and dreams, and had awakened to the truth. I saw it all; I saw her intention. What was I to do?

Without my marking its approach emotion was upon me. The fingers that held up the extended slips tattooed one on another through its negligible thick-ness.

"Pretty thick that," Soane said. He was looking back at me from the cupboard he had opened. "I've rubbed it in, too . . . there'll be hats on the green to-morrow." He had his head inside the cup-board, and his voice came to me hollowly. He ex-tracted a large bottle with a gilt-foiled neck.

"Won't it upset the apple cart to-morrow," he said, very loudly; "won't it?"

His voice acted on me as the slight shake upon a phial full of waiting chemicals; crystallised them suddenly with a little click. Everything suddenly grew very clear to me. I suddenly understood that all the tortuous intrigue hinged upon what I did in the next few minutes. It rested with me now to stretch out my hand to that button in the wall or to let the whole world—"the . . . the probity . . . that sort of thing," she had said—fall to pieces. The drone of the presses continued to make itself felt like the quiver of a suppressed emotion. I might stop them or I might not. It rested with me.

Everybody was in my hands; they were quite small. If I let the thing go on, they would be done for utterly, and the new era would begin.

Soane had got hold of a couple of long-stalked glasses. They clinked together whilst he searched the cupboard for something.

"Eh, what?" he said. "It *is* pretty *strong*, isn't it? Ought to shake out some of the supporters, eh? Bill comes on to-morrow . . . do for that, I should think." He wanted a cork-screw very badly.

But that was precisely it—it would "shake out some of the supporters," and give Gurnard his patent excuse. Churchill, I knew, would stick to his line, the saner policy. But so many of the men who had stuck to Churchill would fall away now, and Gurnard, of course, would lead them to his own triumph.

It was a criminal verdict. Callan had gone out as a commissioner—with a good deal of drum-beating. And this was his report, this shriek. If it sounded across the house-tops—if I let it—good-by to the saner policy and to Churchill. It did not make any difference that Churchill's *was* the saner policy, because there was no one in the nation sane enough to see it. They wanted purity in high places, and here was a definite, criminal indictment against de Mersch. And de Mersch would—in a manner of speaking, have to be lynched, policy or no policy.

She wanted this, and in all the earth she was the only desirable thing. If I thwarted her—she would . . . what would she do now? I looked at Soane.

"What would happen if I stopped the presses?" I asked. Soane was twisting his cork-screw in the wire of the champagne bottle.

It was fatal; I could see nothing on earth but her. What else was there in the world. Wine? The light of the sun? The wind on the heath? Honour! My God, what was honour to me if I could see nothing but her on earth? Would honour or wine or sun or wind ever give me what she could give? Let them go.

"What would happen if what?" Soane grumbled. "*D—n* this wire."

"Oh, I was thinking about something," I answered. The wire gave with a little snap and he began to ease the cork. Was I to let the light pass me by for the sake of . . . of Fox, for instance, who trusted me? Well, let Fox go. And Churchill and what Churchill stood for; the probity; the greatness and the spirit of the past from which had sprung my conscience and the consciences of the sleeping millions around me—the woman at the poultry show with her farmers and shop-keepers. Let them go too.

Soane put into my hand one of his charged glasses. He seemed to rise out of the infinite, a forgotten shape. I sat down at the desk opposite him.

"Deuced good idea," he said, suddenly, "to stop the confounded presses and spoof old Fox. He's up to some devilry. And, by Jove, I'd like to get my knife in him; Jove, I would. And then chuck up everything and leave for the Sandwich Islands. I'm sick of this life, this dog's life. . . . One might have made a pile though, if one'd known this smash was coming. But one can't get at the innards of things.—No such luck—no such luck, eh?" I looked at him stupidly; took in his blood-shot eyes and his ruffled grizzling hair. I wondered who he was. "*Il s'agissait de* . . .?" I seemed to be back in Paris, I couldn't think of what I had been thinking of. I drank his glass of wine and he filled me another. I drank that too.

Ah yes—even then the thing wasn't settled, even now that I had recognised that Fox and the others were of no account . . . What remained was to prove to her that I wasn't a mere chattel, a piece in the game. I was at the very heart of the thing. After all, it was chance that had put me there, the blind chance of all the little things that lead in the inevitable, the future. If, now, I thwarted her, she would . . . what would she do? She would have to begin all over again. She wouldn't want to be revenged; she wasn't revengeful. But how if she would never look upon me again?

The thing had reduced itself to a mere matter of policy. Or was it passion?

A clatter of the wheels of heavy carts and of the hoofs of heavy horses on granite struck like hammer blows on my ears, coming from the well of the court-yard below. Soane had finished his bottle and was walking to the cupboard. He paused at the window and stood looking down.

"Strong beggars, those porters," he said; "I couldn't carry that weight of paper—not with my rot on it, let alone Callan's. You'd think it would break down the carts."

I understood that they were loading the carts for the newspaper mails. There was still time to stop them. I got up and went toward the window, very swiftly. I was going to call to them to stop loading. I threw the casement open.

Of course, I did not stop them. The solution flashed on me with the breath of the raw air. It was ridiculously simple. If I thwarted her, well, she would respect me. But her business in life was the in-heritance of the earth, and, however much she might respect me—or by so much the more—she would

recognise that I was a force to deflect her from the
right line—"a disease for me," she had said.

"What I have to do," I said, "is to show her that
. . . that I had her in my hands and that I co-
operated loyally."

The thing was so simple that I triumphed;
triumphed with the full glow of wine, triumphed looking down into that murky court-yard where the lan-
thorns danced about in the rays of a great arc lamp.
The gilt letters scattered all over the windows blazed
forth the names of Fox's innumerable ventures.   Well,
he   .   .   .   he had been a power, but I triumphed.   I
had co-operated loyally with the powers of the future,
though I wanted no share in the inheritance of the
earth.   Only, I was going to push into the future.   One
of the great carts got into motion amidst a shower of
sounds that whirled upward round and round the well.
The black hood swayed like the shoulders of an ele-
phant as it passed beneath my feet under the arch.
It disappeared—it was co-operating too; in a few hours
people at the other end of the country—of the world—
would be raising their hands.   Oh, yes, it was co-
operating loyally.

I closed the window.   Soane was holding a
champagne bottle in one hand.   In the other he had a
paper knife of Fox's—a metal thing, a Japanese dagger
or a Deccan knife.   He sliced the neck off the bottle.

"Thought you were going to throw yourself out," he
said; "I wouldn't stop you.   *I'm* sick of it   .   .   .
sick."

"Look at this   .   .   .   to-night   .   .   .   this infernal trick of Fox's   .   .   .   And I helped too   .   .   .
Why?   .   .   .   I must eat."   He paused   ".   .   .   and
drink," he added.   "But there is starvation for no end
of fools in this little move.   A few will be losing their

good names too . . . I don't care, I'm off . . . By-the-bye: What is he doing it for? Money? Funk?—You ought to know. You must be in it too. It's not hunger with you. Wonderful what people will do to keep their pet vice going . . . Eh?" He swayed a little. "You don't drink—what's your pet vice?"

He looked at me very defiantly, clutching the neck of the empty bottle. His drunken and overbearing glare seemed to force upon me a complicity in his squalid bargain with life, rewarded by a squalid freedom. He was pitiful and odious to my eyes; and somehow in a moment he appeared menacing.

"You can't frighten me," I said, in response to the strange fear he had inspired. "No one can frighten me now." A sense of my inaccessibility was the first taste of an achieved triumph. I had done with fear. The poor devil before me appeared infinitely remote. He was lost; but he was only one of the lost; one of those that I could see already overwhelmed by the rush from the flood-gates opened at my touch. He would be destroyed in good company; swept out of my sight together with the past they had known and with the future they had waited for. But he was odious. "I am done with you," I said.

"Eh; what? . . . Who wants to frighten? . . . I wanted to know what's your pet vice . . . Won't tell? You might safely—I'm off . . . No . . . Want to tell me mine? . . . No time . . . I'm off . . . Ask the policeman . . . crossing sweeper will do . . . I'm going."

"You will have to," I said.

"What . . . Dismiss me? . . . Throw the indispensable Soane overboard like a squeezed lemon? . . . Would you? . . . What would Fox say?

. . . Eh? But you can't, my boy—not you. Tell
you . . . tell you . . . can't . . . Be-
forehand with you . . . sick of it . . . I'm
off . . . to the Islands—the Islands of the Blest
. . . I'm going to be an . . . no, not an angel
like Fox . . . an . . . oh, a beachcomber.
Lie on white sand, in the sun . . . blue sky and
palm-trees—eh? . . . S.S. *Waikato*. I'm off
. . . Come too . . . lark . . . dismiss
yourself out of all this. Warm sand, warm, mind
you . . . you won't?" He had an injured expression. "Well, I'm off. See me into the cab, old
chap, you're a decent fellow after all . . . not one
of these beggars who would sell their best friend . . .
for a little money . . . or some woman. Will see
the last of me . . ."

I didn't believe he would reach the South Seas, but
I went downstairs and watched him march up the
street with a slight stagger under the pallid dawn. I
suppose it was the lingering chill of the night that made
me shiver. I felt unbounded confidence in the future,
there was nothing now between her and me. The
echo of my footsteps on the flagstones accompanied me,
filling the empty earth with the sound of my progress.

CHAPTER EIGHTEEN

I WALKED along, got to my club and upstairs into my room peaceably. A feeling of entire tranquillity had come over me. I rested after a strife which had issued in a victory whose meaning was too great to comprehend and enjoy at once. I only knew that it was great because there seemed nothing more left to do. Everything reposed within me—even conscience, even memory, reposed as in death. I had risen above them, and my thoughts moved serenely as in a new light, as men move in sunshine above the graves of the forgotten dead. I felt like a man at the beginning of a long holiday—an indefinite space of idleness with some great felicity—a felicity too great for words, too great for joy—at the end. Everything was delicious and vague; there were no shapes, no persons. Names flitted through my mind—Fox, Churchill, my aunt; but they were living people seen from above, flitting in the dusk, without individuality; things that moved below me in a valley from which I had emerged. I must have been dreaming of them.

I know I dreamed of her. She alone was distinct among these shapes. She appeared dazzling; resplendent with a splendid calmness, and I braced myself to the shock of love, the love I had known, that all men had known; but greater, transcendental, almost terrible, a fit reward for the sacrifice of a whole past. Suddenly she spoke. I heard a sound like the rustling of a wind through trees, and I felt the shock of an unknown emotion made up of fear and of enthusiasm, as though she had been not a woman but only a voice crying strange, unknown words in inspiring tones, promising and cruel, without any passion of love or hate. I listened. It was like the wind in the trees of a little wood. No hate . . . no love. No love. There was a crash as of a falling temple. I was borne to the earth, overwhelmed, crushed by an immensity of ruin and of sorrow. I opened my eyes and saw the sun shining through the window-blinds.

I seem to remember I was surprised at it. I don't know why. Perhaps the lingering effect of the ruin in the dream, which had involved sunshine itself. I liked it though, and lay for a time enjoying the—what shall I say?—usualness of it. The sunshine of yesterday— of to-morrow. It occurred to me that the morning must be far advanced, and I got up briskly, as a man rises to his work. But as soon as I got on my legs I felt as if I had already over-worked myself. In reality there was nothing to do. All my muscles twitched with fatigue. I had experienced the same sensations once after an hour's desperate swimming to save myself from being carried out to sea by the tide.

No. There was nothing to do. I descended the staircase, and an utter sense of aimlessness drove me out through the big doors, which swung behind me without noise. I turned toward the river, and on the broad embankment the sunshine enveloped me, friendly, familiar, and warm like the care of an old friend. A black dumb barge drifted, clumsy and empty, and the solitary man in it wrestled with the heavy sweep, straining his arms, throwing his face up to the sky at every effort. He knew what he was doing, though it was the river that did his work for him.

His exertions impressed me with the idea that I too had something to do. Certainly I had. One always has. Somehow I could not remember. It was intolerable, and even alarming, this blank, this emptiness of the many hours before night came again, till suddenly, it dawned upon me I had to make some extracts in the British Museum for our "Cromwell." Our Cromwell. There was no Cromwell; he had lived, had worked for the future—and now he had ceased to exist. His future—our past, had come to an end. The barge with the man still straining at the oar had gone out of sight under the arch of the bridge, as through a gate into another world. A bizarre sense of solitude stole upon me, and I turned my back upon the river as empty as my day. Hansoms, broughams, streamed with a continuous muffled roll of wheels and a beat of hoofs. A big dray put in a note of thunder and a clank of chains. I found myself curiously unable to understand what possible purpose remained to keep them in motion. The past that had made them had come to an end, and their future had been devoured by a new conception. And what of Churchill? He, too, had worked for the future; he would live on, but he had already ceased to exist. I had evoked him in this poignant thought and he came not alone. He came with a train of all the vanquished in this stealthy, unseen contest for an immense stake in which I was one of the victors. They crowded upon me. I saw Fox, Polehampton, de Mersch himself, crowds of figures without a name, women with whom I had fancied myself in love, men I had shaken by the hand, Lea's reproachful, ironical face. They were near; near enough to touch; nearer. I did not only see them, I absolutely felt them all. Their tumultuous and silent stir seemed to raise a tumult in my breast.

I sprang suddenly to my feet—a sensation that I had had before, that was not new to me, a remembered fear, had me fast; a remembered voice seemed to speak clearly incomprehensible words that had moved me before. The sheer faces of the enormous buildings near at hand seemed to topple forward like cliffs in an earthquake, and for an instant I saw beyond them into unknown depths that I had seen into before. It was as if the shadow of annihilation had passed over them beneath the sunshine. Then they returned to rest; motionless, but with a changed aspect.

"This is too absurd," I said to myself. "I am not well." I was certainly unfit for any sort of work. "But I must get through the day somehow." To-morrow . . . to-morrow . . . I had a pale vision of her face as it had appeared to me at sunset on the first day I had met her.

I went back to my club—to lunch, of course. I had no appetite, but I was tormented by the idea of an interminable afternoon before me. I sat idly for a long time. Behind my back two men were talking.

"Churchill . . . oh, no better than the rest. He only wants to be found out. If I've any nose for that sort of thing, there's something in the air. It's absurd to be told that he knew nothing about it. . . . You've seen the *Hour?*" I got up to go away, but suddenly found myself standing by their table.

"You are unjust," I said. They looked up at me together with an immense surprise. I didn't know them and I passed on. But I heard one of them ask:

"Who's that fellow?" . . .

"Oh—Etchingham Granger . . ."

"Is he queer?" the other postulated.

I went slowly down the great staircase. A knot of men was huddled round the tape machine; others came, half trotting, half walking, to peer over heads, under arm-pits.

"What's the matter with that thing?" I asked of one of them.

"Oh, Grogram's up," he said, and passed me. Someone from a point of vantage read out:

"The Leader of the House (Sir C. Grogram, Devonport) said that . . ." The words came haltingly to my ears as the man's voice followed the jerks of the little instrument ". . . the Government obviously could not . . . alter its policy at . . . eleventh hour . . . at dictates of . . . quite irresponsible person in one of . . . the daily . . . papers."

I was wondering whether it was Soane or Callan who was poor old Grogram's "quite irresponsible person," when I caught the sound of Gurnard's name. I turned irritably away. I didn't want to hear that fool read out the words of that . . . It was like the warning croak of a raven in an old ballad.

I began desultorily to descend to the smoking-room. In the Cimmerian gloom of the stairway the voice of a pursuer hailed me.

"I say, Granger! I say, Granger!"

I looked back. The man was one of the rats of the lower journalism, large-boned, rubicund, asthmatic; a mass of flesh that might, to the advantage of his country and himself, have served as a cavalry trooper. He puffed stertorously down toward me.

"I say, I say," his breath came rattling and wheezing. "What's up at the *Hour?*"

"I'm sure I don't know," I answered curtly.

"They said you took it yesterday. You've been playing the very devil, haven't you? But I suppose it was not off your own bat?"

"Oh, I never play off my own bat," I answered.

"Of course I don't want to intrude," he said again. In the gloom I was beginning to discern the workings of the tortured apoplectic face. "But, I say, what's de Mersch's little game?"

"You'd better ask him," I answered. It was incredibly hateful, this satyr's mask in the dim light.

"He's not in London," it answered, with a wink of the creased eyelids, "but I suppose, now, Fox and de Mersch haven't had a row, now, have they?"

I did not answer. The thing was wearily hateful, and this was only the beginning. Hundreds more would be asking the same question in a few minutes.

The head wagged on the mountainous shoulders.

"Looks fishy," he said. I recognised that to force words from me, he was threatening a kind of blackmail. Another voice began to call from the top of the stairs—

"I say, Granger! I say, Granger . . ."

I pushed the folding-doors apart and went slowly down the gloomy room. I heard the doors swing again, and footsteps patter on the matting behind me. I did not turn; the man came round me and looked at my face. It was Polehampton. There were tears in his eyes.

"I say," he said, "I say, what does it mean; *what* does it mean?" It was very difficult for me to look at him. "I tell you . . ." he began again. He had the dictatorial air of a very small, quite hopeless man, a man mystified by a blow of unknown provenance. "I tell you . . ." he began again.

"But what has it to do with me?" I said roughly.

"Oh, but *you* . . . you advised me to buy." He had become supplicatory. "Didn't you, now? . . . Didn't you . . . You said, you remember

. . . that . . ." I didn't answer the man.
What had I got to say? He remained looking intently at me, as if it were of the greatest moment to
him that I should make the acknowledgment and
share the blame—as if it would take an immense load
from his shoulders. I couldn't do it; I hated him.

"Didn't you," he began categorically; "didn't you
advise me to buy those debentures of de Mersch's?"
I did not answer.

"What does it all mean?" he said again. "If this
bill doesn't get through, I tell you I shall be ruined.
And they say that Mr. Gurnard is going to smash it.
They are all saying it, up there; and that you—you on
the *Hour* . . . are . . . are responsible." He
took out a handkerchief and began to blow his nose. I
didn't say a single word.

"But what's to be done?" he started again; "what's
to be *done* . . . I tell you . . . My daughter,
you know, she's very brave, she said to me this morning
she could work; but she couldn't, you know; she's not
been brought up to that sort of thing . . . not
even typewriting . . . and so . . . we're all
ruined . . . everyone of us. And I've more than
fifty hands, counting Mr. Lea, and they'll all have to
go. It's horrible . . . I trusted you, Granger, you
know; I trusted you, and they say up there that
you . . ." I turned away from him. I couldn't
bear to see the bewildered fear in his eyes. "So many
of us," he began again, "everyone I know . . . I
told them to buy and . . . But you might have
let us know, Granger, you might have. Think of my
poor daughter."

I wanted to say something to the man, wanted to
horribly; but there wasn't anything to say—not a
word. I was sorry. I took up a paper that sprawled

on one of the purple ottomans. I stood with my back to this haggard man and pretended to read.

I noticed incredulously that I was swaying on my legs. I looked round me. Two old men were asleep in armchairs under the gloomy windows. One had his head thrown back, the other was crumpled forward into himself; his frail, white hand just touched the floor. A little further off two young men were talking; they had the air of conspirators over their empty coffee cups.

I was conscious that Polehampton had left me, that he had gone from behind me; but I don't think I was conscious of the passage of time. God knows how long I stood there. Now and then I saw Polehampton's face before my eyes, with the panic-stricken eyes, the ruffled hair, the lines of tears seaming the cheeks, seeming to look out at me from the crumple of the paper that I held. I knew too, that there were faces like that everywhere; everywhere, faces of panic-stricken little people of no more account than the dead in graveyards, just the material to make graveyards, nothing more; little people of absolutely no use but just to suffer horribly from this blow coming upon them from nowhere. It had never occurred to me at the time that their inheritance had passed to me . . . to us. And yet, I began to wonder stupidly, what was the difference between me to-day and me yesterday. There wasn't any, not any at all. Only to-day I had nothing more to do.

The doors at the end of the room flew open, as if burst by a great outcry penetrating from without, and a man appeared running up the room—one of those men who bear news eternally, who catch the distant clamour and carry it into quiet streets. Why did he disturb me? Did I want to hear his news? I wanted to

think of Churchill; to think of how to explain. . . .
The man was running up the room.

"I say . . . I say, you beggars . . ."

I was beginning to wonder how it was that I felt such absolute conviction of being alone, and it was then, I believe, that in this solitude that had descended upon my soul I seemed to see the shape of an approaching Nemesis. It is permitted to no man to break with his past, with the past of his kind, and to throw away the treasure of his future. I began to suspect I had gained nothing; I began to understand that even such a catastrophe was possible. I sat down in the nearest chair. Then my fear passed away. The room was filling; it hummed with excited voices. "Churchill! No better than the others," I heard somebody saying. Two men had stopped talking. They were middle-aged, a little gray, and ruddy. The face of one was angry, and of the other sad. "He wanted only to be found out. What a fall in the mud." "No matter," said the other, "one is made a little sad. He stood for everything I had been pinning my faith to." They passed on. A brazen voice bellowed in the distance. "The greatest fall of any minister that ever was." A tall, heavy journalist in a white waistcoat was the centre of a group that turned slowly upon itself, gathering bulk. "Done for—stood up to the last. I saw him get into his brougham. The police had a job . . . There's quite a riot down there . . . Pale as a ghost. Gurnard? Gurnard magnificent. Very cool and in his best form. Threw them over without as much as a wink. Outraged conscience speech. Magnificent. Why it's the chance of his life." . . . And then for a time the voices and the faces seemed to pass away and die out. I had dropped my paper, and as I stooped to pick it up the voice returned

—"Granger . . . Etchingham Granger . . .
Sister is going to marry Gurnard."

I got on to my hands and knees to pick up the paper,
of course. What I did not understand was where the
water came from. Otherwise it was pretty clear.
Somebody seemed to be in a fit. No, he wasn't drunk;
look at his teeth. What did they want to look at his
teeth for; was he a horse?

It must have been I that was in the fit. There were
a lot of men round me, the front row on their knees—
holding me, some of them. A man in a red coat and
plush breeches—a waiter—was holding a glass of
water; another had a small bottle. They were talking
about me under their breaths. At one end of the
horseshoe someone said:

"He's the man who . . ." Then he caught
my eye. He lowered his voice, and the abominable
whisper ran round among the heads. It was easy to
guess: "the man who was got at." I was to be that for
the rest of my life. I was to be famous at last. There
came the desire to be out of it.

I struggled to my feet.

Someone said: "Feel better now?" I answered:
"I—oh, I've got to go and see . . ."

It was rather difficult to speak distinctly; my tongue
got in the way. But I strove to impress the fool with
the idea that I had affairs that must be attended to—
that I had private affairs.

"You aren't fit. Let me . . ."

I pushed him roughly aside—what business was it of
his? I slunk hastily out of the room. The others
remained. I knew what they were going to do—to
talk things over, to gabble about "the man who . . ."

It was treacherous walking, that tessellated pavement in the hall. Someone said: "Hullo, Granger," as I passed. I took no notice.

Where did I wish to go to? There was no one who could minister to me; the whole world had resolved itself into a vast solitary city of closed doors. I had no friend—no one. But I must go somewhere, must hide somewhere, must speak to someone. I mumbled the address of Fox to a cabman. Some idea of expiation must have been in my mind; some idea of seeing the thing through, mingled with that necessity for talking to someone—any one.

I was afraid too; not of Fox's rage; not even of anything that he could do—but of the sight of his despair. He had become a tragic figure.

I reached his flat and I had said: "It is I," and again, "It is I," and he had not stirred. He was lying on the sofa under a rug, motionless as a corpse. I had paced up and down the room. I remember that the pile of the carpet was so long that it was impossible to walk upon it easily. Everything else in the room was conceived in an exuberance of luxury that now had something of the macabre in it. It was that now—before, it had been unclean. There was a great bed whose lines suggested sinking softness, a glaring yellow satin coverlet, vast, like a sea. The walls were covered with yellow satin, the windows draped with lace worth a king's ransom, the light was softened, the air dead, the sounds hung slumbrously. And, in the centre of it, that motionless body. It stirred, pivoted on some central axis beneath the rug, and faced me sitting. There was no look of enquiry in the bloodshot eyes— they turned dully upon me, topaz-coloured in a blood-red setting. There was no expression in the suffused face.

"You want?" he said, in a voice that was august by dint of hopelessness.

"I want to explain," I said. I had no idea that this was what I had come for.

He answered only: "You!" He had the air of one speaking to something infinitely unimportant. It was as if I had no inkling of the real issue.

With a bravery of desperation I began to explain that I hadn't stumbled into the thing; that I had acted open-eyed; for my own ends . . . "My own ends." I repeated it several times. I wanted him to understand, and I did explain. I kept nothing from him; neither her coming, nor her words, nor my feelings. I had gone in with my eyes open.

For the first time Fox looked at me as if I were a sentient being. "Oh, you know that much," he said listlessly.

"It's no disgrace to have gone under to her," I said; "we *had* to." His despair seemed to link him into one "we" with myself. I wanted to put heart into him. I don't know why.

He didn't look at me again.

"Oh, *that*," he said dully, "I—I understand who you mean . . . If I had known before I might have done something. But she came of a higher plane." He seemed to be talking to himself. The half-forgotten horror grew large; I remembered that she had said that Fox, like herself, was one of a race apart, that was to supersede us—Dimensionists. And, when I looked at him now, it was plain to me that he *was* of a race different from my own, just as he had always seemed different from any other man. He had had a different tone in triumph; he was different now, in his despair. He went on: "I might have managed Gurnard alone, but I never thought of her coming. You see one does one's best, but, somehow, here one grows rather blind. I ought to have stuck to Gurnard, of course; never to have broken with him. We ought all to have kept together.—But I kept my end up as long as he was alone."

He went on talking in an expressionless monotone, perhaps to himself, perhaps to me. I listened as one listens to unmeaning sounds—to that of a distant train at night. He was looking at the floor, his mouth moving mechanically. He sat perfectly square, one hand on either knee, his back bowed out, his head drooping forward. It was as if there were no more muscular force in the whole man—as if he were one of those ancient things one sees sunning themselves on benches by the walls of workhouses.

"But," I said angrily, "it's not all over, you can make a fight for it still."

"You don't seem to understand," he answered, "it *is* all over—the whole thing. I ran Churchill and his conscious rectitude gang for all they were worth . . . Well, I liked them, I was a fool to give way to pity.— But I did.—One grows weak among people like you. Of course I knew that their day was over . . . And it's all *over*," he said again after a long pause.

"And what will you *do?*" I asked, half hysterically.

"I don't just know," he answered; "we've none of us gone under before. There haven't been enough really to clash until she came."

The dead tranquillity of his manner was overwhelming; there was nothing to be said. I was in the presence of a man who was not as I was, whose standard of values, absolute to himself, was not to be measured by any of mine.

"I suppose I shall cut my throat," he began again.

I noticed with impersonal astonishment that the length of my right side was covered with the dust of a floor. In my restless motions I came opposite the fireplace. Above it hung a number of tiny, jewelled frames, containing daubs of an astonishing lewdness. The riddle grew painful. What kind of a being could conceive this impossibly barbaric room, could enshrine those impossibly crude designs, and then fold his hands? I turned fiercely upon him. "But you are rich enough to enjoy life," I said.

"What's that?" he asked wearily.

"In the name of God," I shouted, "what do you work for—what have you been plotting and plotting for, if not to enjoy your life at the last?" He made a small indefinite motion of ignorance, as if I had propounded to him a problem that he could not solve, that he did not think worth the solving.

It came to me as the confirmation of a suspicion—that motion. They had no joy, these people who were to supersede us; their clear-sightedness did nothing more for them than just that enabling them to spread desolation among us and take our places. It had been in her manner all along, she was like Fate; like the abominable Fate that desolates the whole length of our lives; that leaves of our hopes, of our plans, nothing but a hideous jumble of fragments like those of statues, smashed by hammers; the senseless, inscrutable, joyless Fate that we hate, and that debases us forever and ever. She had been all that to me . . . and to how many more?

"I used to be a decent personality," I vociferated at him. "Do you hear?—decent! I could look a man in the face. And you cannot even enjoy. What do you come for? What do you live for? What is at the end of it all?"

"Ah, if I knew . . ." he answered, negligently.

CHAPTER NINETEEN

I WANTED to see her, to finish it one way or another, and, at my aunt's house, I found her standing in an immense white room; waiting for me. There was a profusion of light. It left her absolutely shadowless, like a white statue in a gallery; inscrutable.

"I have come," I said. I had it in my mind to say: "Because there is nothing for me to do on earth." But I did not, I looked at her instead.

"You have come," she repeated. She had no expression in her voice, in her eyes. It was as if I were nothing to her; as if I were the picture of a man. Well, that was it; I was a picture, she a statue. "I did it," I said at last.

"And you want?" she asked.

"You know," I answered, "I want my . . ." I could not think of the word. It was either a reward or just due. She looked at me, quite suddenly. It made an effect as if the Venus of Milo had turned its head toward me. She began to speak, as if the statue were speaking, as if a passing bell were speaking; recording a passing passionlessly.

"You have done nothing at all," she said. "Nothing."

"And yet," I said, "I was at the heart of it all."

"Nothing at all," she repeated. "You were at the heart, yes; but at the heart of a machine." Her words carried a sort of strong conviction. I seemed suddenly to see an immense machine—unconcerned, soulless, but all its parts made up of bodies of men: a great mill grinding out the dust of centuries; a great wine-press. She was continuing her speech.

"As for you—you are only a detail, like all the

others; you were set in a place because you would act
as you did. It was in your character. We inherit the
earth and you, your day is over . . . You remember that day, when I found you—the first day?''

I remembered that day. It was on the downland,
under the immense sky, amid the sound of larks. She
had explained the nature of things. She had talked
expressionlessly in pregnant words; she was talking now.
I knew no more of her to-day, after all these days, after
I had given up to her my past and my future.

"You remember that day. I was looking for such a
man, and I found you.''

"And you . . ." I said, "you have done this thing!
Think of it! . . . I have nobody—nothing—nowhere
in the world. I cannot look a man in the face, not even
Churchill. I can never go to him again." I paused,
expecting a sign of softening. None came. "I have
parted with my past and you tell me there is no future."

"None," she echoed. Then, coldly, as a swan takes
the water, she began to speak:

"Well, yes! I've hurt you. You have suffered and
in your pain you think me vile, but remember that for
ages the virtue of to-morrow has been the vileness of
to-day. That which outstrips one, one calls vile. My
virtue lies in gaining my end. Pity for you would have
been a crime for me. You have suffered. And then?
What are you to me? As I came among you I am to-
day; that is where I am triumphant and virtuous. I
have succeeded. When I came here I came into a
world of—of shadows of men. What were their
passions, their joys, their fears, their despair, their
outcry to me? If I had ears, my virtue was to close
them to the cries. There was no other way. There
was one of us—your friend Fox, I mean. He came into
the world, but had not the virtue to hold himself aloof.

He has told you, 'One goes blind down here.' He began to feel a little like the people round him. He contracted likings and dislikings. He liked you . . . and you betrayed him. So he went under. He grew blind down here. I have not grown blind. I see as I saw. I move as I did in a world of . . . of the pictures of men. They despair. I hear groans . . . well, they are the groans of the dead to me. This to you, down near it, is a mass of tortuous intrigue; vile in its pettiest detail. But come further off; stand beside me, and what does it look like? It is a mighty engine of disintegration. It has crushed out a whole fabric, a whole plane of society. It has done that. I guided it. I had to have my eyes on every little strand of it; to be forever on the watch.

"And now I stand alone. Yesterday that fabric was everything to you; it seemed solid enough. And where is it to-day? What is it to you more than to me? There stood Virtue . . . and Probity . . . and all the things that all those people stood for. Well, to-day they are gone; the very belief in them is gone. Who will believe in them, now that it is proved that their tools were people . . . like de Mersch? And it was I that did it. That, too, is to be accounted to me for virtue.

"Well, I have inherited the earth. I am the worm at the very heart of the rose of it. You are thinking that all that I have gained is the hand of Gurnard. But it is more than that. It is a matter of a chess-board; and Gurnard is the only piece that remains. And I am the hand that moves him. As for a marriage; well, it is a marriage of minds, a union for a common purpose. But mine is the master mind. As for you. Well, you have parted with your past . . . and there is no future for you. That is true. You have nowhere to go to; have nothing left, nothing in the world. That is true too. But what is that to me? A set of facts— that you have parted with your past and have no future. You had to do the work; I had to make you do it. I chose you because you would do it. That is all . . . I knew you; knew your secret places, your weaknesses. That is my power. I stand for the Inevitable, for the future that goes on its way; you for the past that lies by the roadside. If for your sake I had swerved one jot from my allotted course, I should have been untrue. There was a danger, once, for a minute. . . . But I stood out against it. What would you have had me do? Go under as Fox went under? Speak like him, look as he looks now . . . Me? Well, I did not.

"I was in the hands of the future; I never swerved; I went on my way. I had to judge men as I judged you; to corrupt, as I corrupted you. I cajoled; I bribed; I held out hopes; and with everyone, as with you, I succeeded. It is in that power that the secret of the greatness which is virtue, lies. I had to set about a work of art, of an art strange to you; as strange, as alien as the arts of dead peoples. You are the dead now, mine the art of an ensuing day. All that remains to you is to fold your hands and wonder, as you wondered before the gates of Nineveh. I had to sound the knell of the old order; of your virtues, of your honours, of your faiths, of . . . of altruism, if you like. Well, it is sounded. I was forever on the watch; I foresaw; I forestalled; I have never rested. And you . . ."

"And I . . ." I said, "I only loved you."

There was a silence. I seemed for a moment to see myself a tenuous, bodiless thing, like a ghost in a bottomless cleft between the past and the to come. And I was to be that forever.

"You only loved me," she repeated. "Yes, you loved me. But what claim upon me does that give you? You loved me. . . . Well, if I had loved you it would have given you a claim. . . . All your misery; your heart-ache comes from . . . from love; your love for me, your love for the things of the past, for what was doomed. . . . You loved the others too . . . in a way, and you betrayed them and you are wretched. If you had not loved them you would not be wretched now; if you had not loved me you would not have betrayed your—your very self. At the first you stood alone; as much alone as I. All these people were nothing to you. I was nothing to you. But you must needs love them and me. You should have let them remain nothing to the end. But you did not. What were they to you?—Shapes, shadows on a sheet. They looked real. But were they—any one of them? You will never see them again; you will never see me again; we shall be all parts of a past of shadows. If you had been as I am, you could have looked back upon them unmoved or could have forgotten. . . . But you . . . 'you only loved' and you will have no more ease. And, even now, it is only yourself that matters. It is because you broke; because you were false to your standards at a supreme moment; because you have discovered that your honour will not help you to stand a strain. It is not the thought of the harm you have done the others . . . What are they—what is Churchill who has fallen or Fox who is dead—to you now? It is yourself that you bemoan. That is your tragedy, that you can never go again to Churchill with the old look in your eyes, that you can never go to any one for fear of contempt. . . . Oh, I know you, I know you."

She knew me. It was true, what she said.

I had had my eyes on the ground all this while; now I looked at her, trying to realise that I should never see her again. It was impossible. There was that intense beauty, that shadowlessness that was like translucence. And there was her voice. It was impossible to understand that I was never to see her again, never to hear her voice, after this.

She was silent for a long time and I said nothing—nothing at all. It was the thought of her making Fox's end; of her sitting as Fox had sat, hopelessly, lifelessly, like a man waiting at the end of the world. At last she said: "There is no hope. We have to go our ways; you yours, I mine. And then if you will—if you cannot forget—you may remember that I cared; that, for a moment, in between two breaths, I thought of . . . of failing. That is all I can do . . . for your sake."

That silenced me. Even if I could have spoken to any purpose, I would have held my tongue now.

I had not looked at her; but stood with my eyes averted, very conscious of her standing before me; of her great beauty, of her great glory.

After a long time I went away. I never saw her again. I never saw any one of them all again. Fox was dead and Churchill I have never had the heart to face. That was the end of all that part of my life. It passed away and left me only a consciousness of weakness and . . . and regrets. She remains. One recognises her hand in the trend of events. Well, it is not a very gay world. Gurnard, they say, is the type of the age—of its spirit. And they say that I, the Granger of Etchingham, am not on terms with my brother-in-law.

THE END